"I am willing to pay whatever price you ask—within reason."

"Just like that? You must be completely mad."

"I am altogether sane, I assure you. I would like you to leave, preferably today, but by tomorrow at the latest. And I hope you will give my offer serious consideration."

"It's not worth considering," she said. "It's an insult."

"Your presence here, mademoiselle, is intolerable. Surely you can see that."

"I see nothing of the kind, and I'll leave when I'm ready. And, for the record, I wouldn't touch one *centime* of your rotten money."

He shrugged. "Then I will have to try other methods."

Dear Reader,

We know from your letters that many of you enjoy traveling to foreign locations—especially from the comfort of your favorite chair. Well, sit back and put your feet up as Harlequin Presents concludes its yearlong tour of Europe. **Postcards from Europe** has featured a special title every month during 1994, set in one of your favorite European countries, written by one of your favorite Harlequin Presents authors. We invite you to end our tour in the picturesque region of Périgord, located in the heart of southwest France. Where better to sow the seeds of love than in the fertile soil of an area known for its green fields and lush fruits.

Bon voyage!

The Editors

P.S. Don't miss the fascinating facts we've compiled about France. You'll find them at the end of the story.

HARLEQUIN PRESENTS

Postcards from Europe

SARA CRAVEN

Tower of Shadows

Harlequin Books

TORONTO • NEW YORK • LONDON
AMSTERDAM • PARIS • SYDNEY • HAMBURG
STOCKHOLM • ATHENS • TOKYO • MILAN
MADRID • WARSAW • BUDAPEST • AUCKLAND

ISBN 0-373-11708-6

TOWER OF SHADOWS

Copyright © 1993 by Sara Craven.

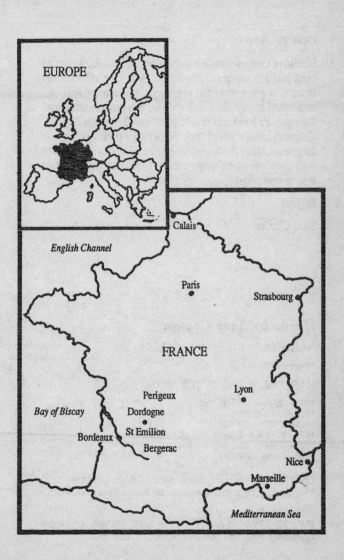

EUROPE

Calais

English Channel

Paris

Strasbourg

FRANCE

Lyon

Perigeux

Dordogne

Bay of Biscay

St Emilion

Bordeaux

Bergerac

Nice

Marseille

Mediterranean Sea

Dear Reader,

I believe that everyone has two countries—their native land and a "country of the heart." My love affair with France began nearly ten years ago. I adore the French esteem of tranquillity and repose; the serious attention they pay to food and drink, which makes even the simplest meal a feast; their respect for their exquisite language; their profound tolerance of children; and the way they take their dogs everywhere with them—even into restaurants!

Enjoy!

Sara Craven

Books by Sara Craven

CHAPTER ONE

SABINE opened the front door with her latch-key and walked into the hall. She stood for a moment, looking round her, waiting for the onrush of some emotion — nostalgia, maybe, or regret. But all she felt was a strange emptiness.

The house, she thought, was like a vacuum, waiting for the personalities of its new owners to fill it.

There's nothing for me here, she told herself. But then, after Maman died, there never really was.

She wished she hadn't come, but Mr Braybrooke had been most insistent.

'You and Miss Russell must meet to discuss the division of the contents. There are still clothes, I understand, and personal items which will need to be disposed of.'

Something in Sabine recoiled from the idea.

She said, 'I suppose — a charity shop.'

'By all means. But surely there will be keepsakes — small pieces of furniture, perhaps, that you will wish to have?'

Sabine shrugged. 'Just Maman's jewellery. She stated in her own will it was to come to me when Dad died.' She paused. 'I'm not sure he would have wanted me to have anything else. There were times during these last couple of years when I felt he hated me. That's why, in the end, I stayed away.'

Mr Braybrooke looked pained. 'But you were Mr Russell's only child, my dear, and you must not doubt that he loved you, even if he didn't always make it perfectly apparent.'

Sabine sighed. 'Be honest, Mr Braybrooke. He left the house, his only tangible asset, jointly to my aunt and myself. I imagine you had to fight like a tiger to secure me even that half of his estate.' She looked at him, brows lifted. 'That's so, isn't it?'

His expression changed to embarrassment. 'I really cannot reveal private discussions with a client.'

Sabine nodded. 'I knew I was right,' she said calmly. 'It's all right, Mr Braybrooke. I've managed to come to terms with it all. I think Dad was the kind of person who could only love one person in his life. He loved Maman, and when she died she took everything. I must have been a constant reminder of her, and he couldn't bear it.'

Mr Braybrooke looked at her for a long moment. Then he said gently, 'I don't think, my dear, that your father was always very wise.'

Standing silent in the hall now, Sabine let herself feel once more the pain of Hugh Russell's rejection of her. Her hands curled slowly into fists, the nails scoring the soft palms until she winced, and let them relax again.

Then squaring her shoulders, she crossed to the drawing-room door, and threw it open.

'So you came.' Aunt Ruth was occupying the wing chair beside the empty grate, her hands busy with the inevitable piece of knitting. Across the room, Sabine could sense her hostility, and wondered how much influence she'd exerted over her brother in those last years.

She said quietly, 'Not by choice, but the house has to be cleared. I see that. When is the sale due to be completed?'

'On Friday.' Ruth Russell's lips were compressed into their usual taut line. 'I've prepared an inventory of the furniture, and ticked those pieces to which I'm particularly attached.'

'That's fine. We can send the remainder to a saleroom.'

Miss Russell stared at her. 'There's nothing you want?'

Sabine glanced round the once familiar room. She had her own flat now, light and bright and filled with the things she herself had carefully chosen. She had her own life. She wanted no hang-ups from the past to shadow the future. And yet. . .

She said, 'Only Maman's jewellery, thank you.'

'That absurd name.' Miss Russell's face showed a sudden, unbecoming flush. 'Take her trinkets. I don't want them.'

'No,' Sabine said meditatively. 'You never liked her, did you?'

'Hugh could have married anyone.' This was clearly an old and bitter theme. 'Instead he chose a foreigner—a girl with no background—no class.'

'The French had a revolution once,' Sabine pointed out mildly. 'It was supposed to wipe out that kind of thinking, and replace it with liberty, equality and brotherhood.' She looked pointedly at the busy hands. 'A lot of knitting went on then, too.'

'You are — insolent.'

'Yes,' Sabine agreed wearily. 'But I tried being polite for a long time, Aunt Ruth, and it got me nowhere. Your dislike for Maman was handed down to me, wasn't it? I often wondered why. I was your brother's child, after all.'

'Oh, no, you were not.'

The words were uttered with such venom that Sabine's head jerked back in shock. She felt as astonished as if the older woman had got out of her chair suddenly, and struck her across the face.

She said, faltering a little, 'What did you say?'

'I said you were not my brother's child.' The words seemed squeezed between the compressed lips. They were staccato with a violence and bitterness which Sabine, stunned, guessed had been suppressed for years. 'Your mother — that precious Maman you speak about with such reverence — was nothing but a common slut. She was already pregnant when Hugh met her. She was living as *au pair* with the Drummonds — such a nice family — and he went there to dinner. Mrs Drummond was distraught when she realised Isabelle's condition. She turned her out of the house, and rightly so — contaminating innocent children.' Her breath rasped harshly.

'She was over six months gone, when he married her,' she went on. 'I begged him on my knees not to do it, but he was besotted with her. He'd never shown the slightest interest in any other woman — any decent woman. Oh, no, he chose her. And everyone knew — everyone was laughing about it.'

Sabine found it difficult to breathe. She tried to

speak calmly. 'You're lying. I know you are. I've seen my birth certificate. My father was Hugh Oliver Russell, however much you may wish to disown the connection.'

'Of course, his name is there. He registered the birth. He claimed you — took responsibility for you. There was no one else to do so. He'd married her, so he accepted the shame of you. She made him do it.'

Sabine's legs were weak suddenly. A chair, she thought. She had to get to a chair otherwise she would collapse on to the floor. She walked somehow to the other side of the fireplace and sat down.

There was no point in argument and denial. She knew that now. Because Ruth Russell was speaking the truth at last, with a furious conviction that left no room for doubt. And although she felt she was being torn apart inside, at the same time the older woman's brutal candour was welcome, because it finally answered so many unhappy questions.

She'd thought she'd failed Hugh Russell in some way, or that she was intrinsically unlovable. Now she knew it wasn't so. It hadn't really involved her personally at all. It was what she represented to him.

Perhaps he'd always secretly resented giving his name to another man's child, she thought sadly. Maybe the fact that she'd remained the only one had rankled with him too.

She said, 'I wish he'd told me this himself.'

'He never would. He was too loyal to *her.*'

Sabine lifted her chin. 'Did he know — who my real father was?'

Ruth Russell shook her head. 'She would never say.

In all those years, she refused to speak about it — to give even a clue.'

'Although I'm sure you never hesitated to badger her about it,' Sabine said evenly.

'We had a right to know whose bastard we were fostering.'

'That's certainly one way of looking at it,' Sabine agreed. She took a breath. 'In the circumstances, I presume you want me to remove all Maman's things from the house.'

'I wanted him to do it after she died. To get rid of everything — every trace of her. But he wouldn't. In spite of what she'd done — even when she was dead — he went on loving her — the blind, stupid fool.' Tears were running down Ruth Russell's face.

'I know,' Sabine said gently. 'And for that reason I shall always love his memory.' She got to her feet. 'I'll make a start upstairs. Goodbye — Miss Russell. There's very little reason for us to meet again.'

'None at all.' The tone was like a knife, severing any tenuous bond that might remain between them.

Sabine wryly decided against any attempt to shake hands, and left the room.

She was still dazed by the revelations of the past half-hour as she went up the stairs. She'd come to perform an unpleasant but routine chore, and suddenly, virtually in the twinkling of an eye, her entire life had been turned upside-down, and all its certainties challenged.

If she shared no blood tie with Hugh Russell, she found herself debating the morality of claiming any part of his estate at all. She would have to talk to Mr Braybrooke about it.

But she wouldn't think about that now. She would concentrate on the job in hand instead, and get it done as quickly and cleanly as possible.

During Isabelle Russell's lifetime, she and her husband had shared the big front bedroom. After her death, he'd moved out into one of the back rooms, and Aunt Ruth — although she supposed she'd have to stop thinking of her in that way — had taken the other.

Fourteen-year-old Sabine had remained in the roomy attic which had been hers since nursery days. It had always been a much loved and private domain. Often, in those anguished and bewildered days as Miss Russell began to impose a new regime, it had become a sanctuary.

Eventually, Sabine had been glad to escape altogether to university, where she'd read Modern Languages. Vacations had proved such a strain that she stopped going home at all in the end, applying for any holiday jobs which offered accommodation. After obtaining her degree, she decided against teaching, opting instead for a career as a freelance translator. So far, she hadn't regretted it.

She was thankful too that she'd struggled to exist on her grant, and what she earned in vacations, without making too many extra demands on Hugh Russell. She'd been well aware that Ruth Russell grudged her every penny.

To her I was always an outsider — an interloper, she thought, as she opened the door of the master bedroom. At least I know why now.

Miss Russell had a morbid fear of sunlight fading carpets and furnishings, so the curtains were half drawn as usual. Sabine wrenched them apart, and opened the windows for good measure, letting the brightness of the June day flood into the room. Then she looked around her.

It was like taking a step back into the past, and for a moment a little shiver ran down her spine. The bed had been stripped, of course, but apart from that everything seemed much the same. Too much the same. She could almost imagine the door opening and Isabelle coming in to sit down at the dressing-table with its pretty antique tortoiseshell and silver toilet set, humming softly as she loved to do.

What was the song which had always been her favourite as a child? Sabine hummed the tune, then sang the words under her breath. '*Auprès de ma blonde, il fait bon, fait bon, fait bon Auprès de ma blonde, il fait bon dormir.*'

A most unsuitable thing to teach a child, Miss Russell had always said disapprovingly. But it had just been part of Isabelle's patient determination to make Sabine as bilingual as possible.

'You have French blood. You must take pride in speaking our beautiful language,' she had told the little girl more than once. And songs, even faintly *risqué* ones about blondes, had been part of the learning process.

Isabelle had been blonde herself, of course, her eyes as dark as brown pansies, in startling contrast to her pale hair and creamy skin.

Sabine had inherited her mother's fair hair, and wore

it sleekly cut in a similar straight bob, swinging almost to her shoulders. She was the same medium height too, with the lithe slenderness which had also characterised Isabelle. But her eyes were greyish-green, and her oval face had charm, rather than the outright beauty which her mother had possessed.

She had always tried to emulate Isabelle, too, in buying the best clothes she could afford, and keeping them in pristine condition, making sure she was well-groomed at all times.

Ruth Russell had claimed her sister-in-law had no class, yet Isabelle could achieve the kind of casual chic which made every other woman around her look dowdy. Probably that had been one of the things which Aunt Ruth, who had little dress sense, so disliked about her.

She stood absently fingering the jars and brushes on the dressing-table. Even when Hugh Russell's attitude towards her had begun to change it had never occurred to her to doubt her parentage for a moment. She'd always believed in the strength of her parents' marriage, the power of its mutual affection. Now she had to face the fact that it could all have been a sham.

Isabelle had loved another man—had given herself to him with disastrous consequences—and here was Sabine, the living proof, the cuckoo in the conventional Russell family nest.

She wondered if Hugh Russell had ever hinted that his wife should have her baby adopted. According to Miss Russell, Isabelle had forced him to treat her child as his own—had even made it a condition of their marriage.

He had loved her, Sabine thought, but how had she felt about him? Was it love or simply gratitude because he had offered her a safe haven? She would never know.

Biting her lip, Sabine walked over to the wardrobe, and flung open its door. They were still hanging there on their plastic covers—the classic suits, the dateless dresses, with the shoes, always plain courts, racked neatly beneath them.

She lifted down the big suitcase from the top of the wardrobe, and, placing it on the bed, began to fill it, folding the garments as carefully as Isabelle would have done.

At times, a faint remembrance of the scent her mother used to wear drifted up from the folds of the clothing. That was the most personally evocative thing of all, Sabine thought, wincing, and she could understand why Hugh had always shied away from clearing out his wife's things. It was interesting too, she realised, that he'd never allowed his sister to dispose of them either.

But then, he wouldn't have wanted to see Isabelle's treasured possessions grimly thrust into bin-bags and left outside for collection.

It took nearly an hour for her to empty the wardrobe and dressing-table. She didn't hurry, using the time to do some serious thinking. It occurred to her for the first time that there were a couple of curious anomalies in her childhood.

Firstly, although Isabelle had kindled her love for foreign languages by teaching her their own native tongue, at the same time she'd been strangely reticent about her own life. When Sabine asked about France and French life, Isabelle had talked exclusively about Paris where she'd trained as a commercial artist. For that reason, Sabine had always assumed that her mother was a Parisienne by birth.

But assumptions, as she'd discovered that day, could be dangerous, and Isabelle had never actually stated where she was born. She'd never spoken about family either. Sabine had asked if she had any grandparents in France, or any other uncles and aunts. It seemed unjust if she was saddled with Aunt Ruth alone, but Isabelle had said there was no one, adding, '*Hélas.*'

The other odd thing, she realised, was that they'd never been on holiday to France. Nor could she recollect that it had ever been suggested they should do so. It was as if the subject had been taboo.

Yet they'd been to Spain, Italy and Greece time after time, and surely it would have been natural for Isabelle to want to show off the country of her birth.

Why did I never think of this before? she wondered blankly. Presumably because I was too young, and because life was so full in other ways that I never had time or any real reason to question it.

She'd left the top dressing-table drawer until last. It still contained a handful of cosmetics, and, at the very back, her mother's suede jewellery case. Sabine extracted it gently. Her mother had been quite specific about it. 'My jewellery case and all its contents to my daughter Sabine', her will had read, with the added proviso that the bequest should only take place after Hugh Russell's own death. Maman's perception had probably told how impossible it would be for him to part with any of her things in his lifetime.

In fact, there was very little inside the case, just her watch, a few pairs of earrings, and her cultured pearl necklace. The tray didn't fit very well, she noticed, and when she lifted it out she discovered why. Under it was a small flat package wrapped in yellowing tissue paper.

Sabine removed the paper carefully, trying not to tear it, feeling in many ways like an intruder. An oval silver medallion and chain slid into her hand, and she studied it, frowning. She knew all Isabelle's small store of jewellery, and she'd certainly never seen this before, although she had to admit it was a beautiful thing. Moreover, it looked old, and by its weight in her hand could also be valuable. And equally clearly, concealed in the base of the box, it had not been for public view.

There was some kind of engraving on the medallion, and she took it over to the window for a closer look. The design wasn't very clear, but she could just make out a building shaped like a tower, she thought, tracing the outline with her fingertip, and beneath it a flower which might or might not be a rose.

Sabine looked at it for a long moment, aware of a faint stirring in her consciousness, some elusive memory, fleetingly brought to life. But as she reached for it, tried to bring it into sharper focus, it was gone. Just another unanswered question, she acknowledged with a small sigh, as she re-wrapped it.

She was about to replace it when she noticed that the satin lining in the bottom of the case had been torn away from one edge, and stitched back into place with large clumsy stitches.

Not Maman's style at all, she thought, frowning. I
wonder when that happened?

She ran her fingers over the base, finding an unexpected bulkiness. There was something there — under
the lining. She found a pair of nail scissors and cut the
stitches.

The something was an elderly manila envelope,
secured with a rubber band.

Slowly Sabine opened it, and emptied the contents
on to the dressing-table. A latch-key attached to a ring
in the shape of a small enamelled owl fell out first to
be followed by a thin folder of photographs, a picture
postcard, a label from a wine bottle, and, lastly, some
kind of official document in French.

It was a mixed bunch, she thought wonderingly.
Rather like that game where you had to memorise so
many objects on a tray.

She picked up the document, and spread it open.
Her heart seemed to be beating very slowly and loudly
as she looked down it. She read it carefully twice, but
her conclusion was the same both times. It was some
kind of title deed to a house in France. A house called
Les Hiboux, sited in the *département* of the Dordogne,
which she knew was in the south-west, near a community called Issigeac. Not that it meant a thing to her.

'*My jewellery case and all its contents to my daughter
Sabine*'.

All its contents.

She felt cold suddenly, and pushed everything back
into the envelope. She would look at the rest later. For
now, she had enough shocks to assimilate, she thought,

as she put the case into her bag, and took a last look round.

She left the envelope on her dining table while she prepared her evening meal. Everywhere she went in the flat, she seemed to catch sight of it out of the corner of her eye. It was not to be ignored.

She'd called at the library on her way home and borrowed some books on the Dordogne. She glanced through them as she ate. The actual region where the house was situated was called the Périgord, and it was divided up into the White, the Green and the Black. Les Hiboux was in the Périgord Noir, which was called that, apparently, because of all the trees, particularly oaks, in the area. It was also a major tourist centre.

Issigeac, she discovered, was south of Bergerac, and on the edge of its wine-growing area.

Part of the Périgord's fame, she read, rested on its cuisine, which included wild mushrooms, *pâté de foie gras*, and the ultimate luxury of truffles. Walnuts were another speciality, cultivated for salad oil, and also for a strong local liqueur.

She made a pot of strong coffee, and reached for the envelope. Les Hiboux, she thought, as the owl keyring fell into her hand. *Hibou* was French for owl. She put it to one side, and opened the folder of photographs.

There weren't many, and they were all black and white. She studied them, frowning. They were just ordinary, rather amateurish snapshots. There were a couple of two children, a girl barely past the toddler stage in a sunbonnet and ruffled dress, and a much older boy, all arms and legs and ferocious scowl, staring pugnaciously at the camera. Maman had given the impression she was an only child, she thought, but was that the truth? Did she have relatives — a real family down in the south-west of France?

The other shots showed a man, standing alone outside some tall stone building. They were blurred and his features were indistinct, but Sabine got the impression that he wasn't particularly young. She glanced at the back of each print, hoping for a name or a date or some other clue, but there was nothing. The man and the children remained anonymous.

She looked at the postcard next, her brows lifting in delight. It depicted a castle in a fairy-tale — a sprawl of golden stone topped by a high, sloping roof, and embellished with turrets. Sabine turned the card over. *'Le Château La Tour Monchauzet'* the printed legend uncompromisingly informed her, with no further elaboration.

The wine label repeated the same words in a floridly ornate script overprinted on a picture, which Sabine recognised instantly. It was a simple drawing of a square tower, standing in splendid isolation like an accusing finger pointing at the sky. And at its base, as if tossed to the ground from one of the tower's high windows, was a highly stylised rose.

It's the same design as the medallion, she thought, with a little lurch of excitement. A tower and a rose. There's definitely something familiar about that — something I recognised before. One of the stories, maybe, that Maman told me when I was small. Oh, why can't I remember? I need to know.

They were a motley collection — these remnants of

her mother's past, she thought, as she began to put them back in the envelope. The deed to the house and the key she could understand — just. But what was the significance of the rest of it?

Well, there was only one way to find out. She was overdue for some leave, and she could go to France and make some enquiries.

But should she? Isabelle might have left her the case, but she'd hidden these things away, making sure they wouldn't be discovered at least while her husband was alive. Clearly she hadn't wanted Hugh to know she owned any property in her native country, but why conceal such an important fact? It made no sense — no sense at all.

Perhaps Isabelle hadn't wanted them found at all, had intended her secret, whatever it was, to die with her.

But that can't be true, Sabine thought, or she'd have burned the lot, and put the key down the nearest drain. No, for good or ill, they were intended for me. And now I have to make a decision.

Les Hiboux. Owls. Birds of ill-omen.

She shivered suddenly, and her arm caught the folder of photographs, knocking it on to the floor. The prints spilled on to the carpet and as Sabine bent to retrieve them the young boy's face seemed to glare directly up at her, challenging and inimical. And she pulled a face back at him.

She said aloud, 'I don't know who you are, but I hope you've mellowed. Or that we never meet. Because you could make a nasty enemy.'

CHAPTER TWO

SABINE brought the car to a halt at the side of the road. She looked across the valley to the thick cluster of trees on the hill opposite, and the tantalising glimpse of pointed grey roofs rising above them in the sunlight. And below the trees, covering the hillside, there were the vines, row upon row of them, like some squat green army.

The Château La Tour Monchauzet, she thought swallowing. Journey's end.

I don't have to do this, she told herself. I could just look — take a photograph perhaps, and then travel on. Put the past behind me, and treat this as an ordinary holiday.

She could, but she knew that she wouldn't. With Mr Braybrooke's astonished help, she'd managed to ascertain that as Isabelle Riquard's only child, Sabine was legal heir to Les Hiboux.

A house in France was a luxury she couldn't afford, but she needed to visit it at least once — to make a reasoned decision about the future of her unexpected inheritance. She'd flown to Bordeaux the previous day, and rented a car at the airport. She'd taken her time, driving down to Bergerac, conscious of the left-hand drive, and unfamiliar road conditions.

'Driving in France is bliss,' everyone had told her. 'Marvellous roads, and half the traffic.'

So far she had to agree. The route from Bordeaux to Bergerac had been straight and fast, and presented her with few problems. And she'd been charmed with Bergerac itself. She'd booked in to a hotel on the Place Gambetta, had a leisurely bath to iron out the kinks of the journey, then followed the receptionist's directions to the old part of the town, a maze of narrow streets where old timbered buildings leaned amiably towards each other.

Although there were plenty of tourists about, mainly British, German and Dutch, Sabine had judged, she had no sense of being in a crowd. There seemed to be space for everyone.

In one square, she'd found a statue of Cyrano de Bergerac, his famous nose sadly foreshortened, probably by vandals, but otherwise much as Rostand had envisaged him.

There were plenty of bars and restaurants to choose from, but Sabine had already mentally opted for a simple meal. She was too much on edge to plunge whole-heartedly into the delights of Périgordian cuisine, she'd decided ruefully.

She had found a traditional-style establishment, full of oak beams and dried flowers, which specialised in meat grilled on an open fire in the restaurant itself. She'd ordered a fillet steak, accompanied by a *gratin dauphinois* and green beans, and while this was being prepared sipped the *apéritif* suggested by the *patronne*, a glass of well-chilled golden Monbazillac wine. It was like tasting honey and flowers, she had thought, beginning perceptibly to relax.

To her disappointment, she had not been able to find

a Château La Tour Monchauzet vintage on the wine-list, but the half-bottle of Côtes de Bergerac that she chose instead more than made up for it.

Once she'd made her decision to come to the Dordogne, Sabine had read up as much as possible on the area, and she knew that Bergerac wines had been overshadowed in the past by the great *vignobles* of Bordeaux.

Bordeaux had not taken kindly to competition from what it dismissed as 'the hinterland', and had even insisted at one point on Bergerac wines being shipped in smaller casks, thus forcing the Bergerac *vignerons* to pay more tax on their exports, the money being levied per cask. But that kind of dirty trick had been relegated firmly to history, and now Bergerac wines had a recognised and growing share of the market.

Before she set off the following morning, she'd visited the Maison du Vin, which was housed in a former medieval monastery. Sabine had been guiltily aware of the click of her sandal heels on the flags of the ancient cloister, and was tempted to tiptoe instead, in case she upset the sleeping spirits of the long-departed monks with such frivolous modernity.

But inside the old building she had found the staff reassuringly up to date, and smilingly efficient.

They had provided her with a local map, pin-pointing the exact location of the Château La Tour Monchauzet, and explaining she should take the Villereal road out of Issigeac, but only for a short distance. Then there would be a signpost. But, they had warned, it was not certain she could tour the château or its vines. It was owned by the Baron de Rochefort and his family, and visitors had not been encouraged for some time, as the *Baron* did not enjoy the best of health. Perhaps it would be wise to telephone first.

However, in the same area, they had added, there were other *vignerons,* who would be happy to show her the wine-making process, using the most modern and scientific methods, and allow her also to taste their products without obligation. They had given her a list.

She was also looking for a house called Les Hiboux. Well, that was more difficult. For serious exploration of the neighbourhood, they recommended a series of small-scale maps, available from any Maison de Presse. The house she sought, if long-established, could well be marked. If not, she could make enquiries at one of the local *mairies*.

Sabine had to admit that the château, tucked among its encircling trees, had the look of a place which actively discouraged visitors. If she hadn't been looking out for the signpost, she could easily have driven past without even realising it was there.

But now it was decision time. Did she turn off on to the single track road across the valley, or take the easy option and drive on towards Villereal?

She glanced at the passenger-seat beside her. The tip of the envelope was just protruding from her bag.

She was probably making a big fuss about very little, said a small voice inside her. Perhaps Isabelle had simply visited the château once as a guest, in the old days, before the *Baron* became ill, and had kept the postcard and label as souvenirs of a happy day. A nice, comfortable thought, she told herself wryly. Only it didn't explain how the medallion came to be in her mother's possession.

Well, there was only one way to find out, she thought, resolutely re-starting the engine.

The road she found herself on was single-track, and twisting. The stream in the bottom of the valley was spanned by a narrow bridge, and she squeezed the car across it, and started up the hill on the other side. The vines spread away on both sides of her, and she could see people working among them, moving slowly along the ranks of greenery.

As she rounded the final corner, the trees were in front of her, a dark and impenetrable barrier hiding the house completely. The road itself ran beneath a tall archway, the gates of which were standing open. One of the high stone pillars carried a large, new-looking sign, showing the château's name, with the now familiar emblem of the tower and the rose beside it.

Underneath was a smaller board which said curtly, '*Privé*'.

Well, she'd been warned not to expect the welcome mat, Sabine thought, as she drove under the arch. The drive up to the château was deeply shadowed by the trees, and Sabine found the gloom trying after the brilliance of the sunshine on the open road. As she peered ahead of her, something shot across the road in front of the car, forcing her to brake sharply. It was probably only a rabbit, but it had still unnerved her slightly, and she pulled off the drive and parked on the grass.

She leaned against the steering-wheel, resting her forehead on her folded arms. She was nervous of her

own shadow today—strung taut as a wire. The problem
was she had no real idea of what she was going to say
or do when she got to the château. Or was she simply
going to drive up to the front door and announce
herself?

'Good day, *messieurs, dames,*' she rehearsed silently.
'I am the daughter of Isabelle Riquard.'

Very impressive, she thought. She could just see the
raised eyebrows, the exchange of bemused glances,
and the shrugs which said, So what? before they
politely but firmly showed her the door. Maybe she
should have listened to the girl at the Maison du Vin
and phoned ahead.

She opened the car door and got out, stretching. It
was cool under the trees, and she could hear birds
singing. The wood seemed to be beckoning to her, but
she resisted the temptation. The last thing she needed
was to be found trespassing in the *Baron*'s private
grounds.

She was just about to get back in the car, when she
heard another vehicle coming up the hill fast. Sabine
had an ignominious impulse to run and hide somewhere. Then she took a deep breath, telling herself not
to be such a fool, and stand her ground. If this was one
of the family, she might have some explaining to do
quite soon, but they couldn't eat her, for heaven's
sake. She leaned against the bonnet of the car and
waited.

With a snarl, a small Peugeot rounded the corner
and headed towards her. Sabine pinned on a polite
smile, and aimed it straight at the oncoming vehicle's
windscreen. Then, just as if the world had frozen and

stopped for a moment, she saw the woman in the driving seat, face white, eyes glassy with shock, the mouth stretched in a grimace which looked like terror.

Sabine cried out in horror as the Peugeot swerved crazily, and plunged off the road. There was the sound of crunching metal as it hit one of the trees a glancing blow and came to a rocking halt.

For a moment Sabine couldn't move. It had all been so fast, she could hardly believe what had happened. All she could think of was the panic on the other woman's face when she'd seen her.

I was just standing there, she thought dazedly. I did nothing to cause that. Nothing.

But there was the Peugeot, its wing crumpled beyond recognition, and still inside was the driver, slumped over the wheel.

'Oh, my God.' Power returned to Sabine's limbs and she dashed frantically across the road, and tugged at the driver's door. It came open at once, and she leaned in, trying to disentangle the unconscious woman from her seatbelt. She'd obviously hit her head during the impact because there was a small trickle of blood on her forehead.

Sabine got the seatbelt off at last, and heaved and dragged the woman, arms and legs trailing, clear of the car. Fortunately, she was petite and thin, almost to the point of emaciation, but all the same Sabine needed all her strength to struggle with her to the grass on the opposite side of the road.

She wasn't a young woman, either. Her hair, drawn back from her face into a chignon, was iron-grey, and there were deep lines around her nose and mouth.

She had the most ghastly pallor, Sabine thought, racing to fetch her jacket from the car and put it under the older woman's head as a pillow. As she did so, the colourless lips moved in a faint moan.

At least she's not dead, Sabine thought, relief flooding through her. She leaned close to the woman's ear and said urgently, 'Don't move, *madame*. I'm going to get help.'

She jumped into her own car, hands fumbling with the ignition key. It started finally at the third attempt, and Sabine was almost weeping as she threw it at the hill. After the next corner, the road divided, and Sabine took the right-hand fork. Almost at once, the road levelled out, and she beat her fist on the steering-wheel in frustration.

'The château's at the very top of the hill,' she wailed to herself. 'This can't be the way.'

She was looking for somewhere to turn when she suddenly realised there were buildings ahead of her. Not a house, but barns or storage areas of some kind. Oh, let there be someone around, she prayed silently, as she made the car fly the last few metres.

Directly ahead of her, three men stood in a group talking. At the sound of her approach, their heads swivelled towards her as if pulled by strings, their expressions transfixed by astonishment and alarm. If she hadn't been so upset, it would almost have been funny.

Sabine tried to brake, stalled instead, and tumbled out of the car. 'Please,' she said between sobbing breaths. 'Please come with me. There's been an accident. A lady has been hurt.'

One of the men strode over to her. Sabine had a confused impression of height and strength, and an anger so powerful that she felt scorched by it.

His hand closed on her arm, bruising her, and she cried out in pain.

'Who are you?' A voice like steel and ice. 'What are you doing here?'

'That doesn't matter now. You've got to help me. Someone's injured.'

He swore violently under his breath, and Sabine found herself being propelled without gentleness into her own passenger-seat. He slotted himself in behind the steering-wheel, and started the car first time. Bastard, she thought. Know-all.

'Show me.'

'It was just before the fork.' In spite of the heat of the day, her teeth had begun to chatter. 'I was standing on the grass—just standing there. She—saw me, and—and—ran into a tree. I—I didn't believe it.'

'No?' There was a kind of savage irony in his voice, and the dark eyes seared her. 'I do.'

The damage to the Peugeot looked even worse as they approached, and Sabine groaned under her breath. The driver was sitting up, holding a hand groggily to her head.

'How did she get there?' Sabine was asked with a curtness that threatened to remove a layer of skin.

'I put her there. I suppose I shouldn't have moved her, but I was worried about the petrol tank—the car exploding.'

But he was already out of the car, ignoring her faltering explanation. He went down on one knee

beside the older woman. 'Tante Héloise.' His voice
had gentled quite magically. 'Keep still, and try to be
calm. Jacques has gone to call an ambulance.'

'No.' A thin hand gestured in agitation. 'It isn't
necessary. I bumped my head, that's all. I don't wish
to go to the hospital. Just take me to the house.'

'You should have treatment. There may be some
concussion.'

'No, Gaston must not be worried.' Her voice was
stronger, more forceful, and she was struggling to get
up. 'Take me home, and send for Dr Arnaud if you
must.'

As he helped her up, her gaze went past to him to
Sabine, who was just getting out of the car to offer her
assistance. The returning colour drained out of her face
again, and she looked on the point of collapse.

'*Mon Dieu!*' she said, her voice hoarse and strained.
'Isabelle.'

Sabine flinched, but she kept her tone low, controlled. 'You are mistaken, *madame*. My mother is
dead.'

The woman cried out, and sagged against the man
holding her, pressing her face against his arm. He
turned his head and glared at Sabine. It was a look she
recognised instantly, although it was the first time she'd
seen it in the flesh. He was the young boy in the
photograph, but over six feet now, with broad
shoulders and lean hips. The scowl too had gained at
least another twenty years of maturity. It had a lethal
edge now which cut her to the bone. She knew she
didn't deserve such scorn, but she felt herself shrink
back, just the same.

'Get in the car, *mademoiselle*.' Contempt scored every word. 'Haven't you done enough harm today? You're not wanted here. Go, and don't come back.'

She was trembling all over, holding on to the car door for support, despising herself for her own weakness. Dry-mouthed, she said, 'I would—only I don't think I can drive just yet.' She lifted her chin, glaring back, refusing to allow herself to be bested completely. 'Or do you want to sacrifice another tree?'

For a long moment their glances clashed like swords, then there was a shout behind her, and she turned to see the two men he'd been talking to and a short stout woman in a dark overall running towards them.

'Jacques.' One of the men was singled out with an imperative finger, which was then stabbed at Sabine. 'Take her wherever she wants to go. Only get her off this estate now, you understand? Before more damage is done,' he added in an undertone.

It was unjust and degrading to be hustled away like this, Sabine thought. She'd had a shock herself. She'd rescued this woman—his aunt presumably—from her crashed car, and gone for help. So much for gratitude— and the much vaunted French hospitality, she thought almost hysterically as Jacques, his face expressionless, indicated that she should resume her seat in the car.

She looked back, and saw that Tante Héloïse was being led away on the arm of the stout woman.

He was examining the damage to the Peugeot, and didn't even glance in the direction of the departing car.

She sank back into her seat, still trembling. She hadn't expected to be greeted with open arms, but the reception she'd actually received had shaken her to the core. Isabelle must have left a legacy of frightening bitterness behind her in this place in order to set off a reaction like that.

She found it totally incomprehensible. She tried to remember Isabelle objectively—wondering how she would have regarded her if they had simply met as strangers, but all she could call to mind was her mother's warmth, and gentleness and capacity for love, and a slow anger began to build in her. She could excuse Ruth Russell to a certain extent. She was a jealous and overly possessive woman who would have loathed anyone her brother had married.

But there was no defence to be made out for the people she'd met today. The small voice inside her, urging her to cut her losses and go back to England, leaving the residents at the Château La Tour Monchauzet to stew in their own rancour, was being overwhelmed by a furious determination to vindicate her mother's memory at all costs.

I'm not going to hang my head and run, she told herself. Nor will I be treated like—a pariah. They may have driven my mother away, but they won't get rid of me so easily.

Jacques slowed the car for the bridge. 'Where do you wish to be taken, *mademoiselle*?' he asked with chill formality. 'You have arranged accommodation?'

She'd noticed an attractive country hotel on her way through Issigeac, and thought she might as well return there. Her lips parted to tell him so, and then she heard herself say, to her own amazement, 'Take me to Les Hiboux, please.'

His head jerked round to look at her, and he missed

a gear change. 'Les Hiboux?' he repeated. 'But that is an empty house.'

She said coolly, 'Which I believe belonged to my mother, Isabelle Riquard.'

'Why, yes, but——'

'I intend to use it,' she cut across him flatly. 'Is it far from here?'

Jacques would normally, she guessed, have an open, cheerful face, on the borderline of good-looking, but now he looked distinctly glum.

'No, not far. But M'sieur Rohan would not wish. . .' He hesitated in turn. 'It would be better, *mademoiselle*, for me to take you to the nearest *syndicat d'initiative*. Someone there will be able to arrange a room for you. It would be wiser, believe me.'

She could guess the identity of M'sieur Rohan only too well, and steel entered her voice. 'And I prefer to stay at Les Hiboux. If you won't take me, then stop the car here, and I'll find my own way.'

His mouth tightened. 'The *patron*, *mademoiselle*, instructed me to drive you wherever you wished to go. And that is what I shall do.'

Jacques called this Monsieur Rohan 'the boss', but surely that didn't mean he was the Baron de Rochefort? The girl at the Maison du Vin had said the *Baron* was in poor health, and this—Rohan looked capable of strangling tigers with his bare hands.

The thought of him—the way he'd looked at her, and spoken—made her start to shake again, but this time with temper. She looked out of the car window, struggling to regain her composure.

In other circumstances, this would have been a

pleasant drive. Freed from the necessity to concentrate on the road, she could have admired the sweep of the rolling scenery of broad fields dotted with cattle, and tree-crowned hills. There were a few houses here and there, some clearly centuries old, their stones weathered to a cream, and pale sand, dark shutters closed against the power of the south-western sun. Others were distinctly modern, looking sharp and raw against the soft colours of their rural backdrop, but all were built with the steeply sloping roofs and heavy timbering that she'd already come to recognise as typical of the region. She remembered reading that all kinds of property, as well as building land in the Dordogne area, was being snapped up by the British and the Dutch.

But the only real sign of activity she could see were the tractors, at work in some of the fields, cutting hay. Certainly, they'd passed no other vehicles.

It was totally tranquil, utterly serene, stamped with an ageless certainty and stability, and, for the first time, Sabine realised what poets had meant when they sang of *'La Douce France'*.

I belong here, she thought fiercely. They won't send me away.

They had turned on to a side-road now. In the fields on both sides, the grass grew high, interspersed with the crimson splash of poppies. They passed a grey stone workshop selling agricultural machines, a small garage with two petrol pumps, and a war memorial surmounted by a statue of Christ on the cross.

They turned again on to an even narrower track, its tarmac pitted and holed, with grass growing down the centre of it. Far ahead of her, Sabine could see a cluster of buildings, obviously a farm, but on her left, set back from the road across an expanse of roughly cropped grass and stones, was a smaller property, whitewashed walls, and earth-red tiles, standing alone.

She did not need Jacques's laconic, 'We have arrived, *mademoiselle,*' to tell her that this was Les Hiboux. Somehow, she already knew.

The house presented a defensive, almost secretive face to the world, she thought, as they approached. Fronting the road was a long wall bisected by a low archway, and terminated by a structure like a squat tower, surmounted by the usual pointed roof. As far as she could see, the rest of the house seemed to be single-storeyed. She reached for her bag, her hand closing on the bunch of keys, as Jacques brought the car to a halt.

They both got out, and he looked at her, his pleasant face serious, even concerned. 'You wish me to come with you — to make sure all is well?'

'Thank you, but no.' She needed to be alone for this. 'How — how are you going to get back to the château? Do you want to borrow the car and return it later?'

'There is no problem,' he assured her. 'By the road, it seems a long way, but I need only to walk a kilometre across the fields beyond the farm. It is nothing.'

Following his indication, Sabine realised with a hollow feeling that all they'd done was skirt the hill where the château stood; that Les Hiboux in fact stood beneath La Tour Monchauzet, but on its other side — and still in its shadow.

I could have done without that, she thought, and the short-cut past the farm.

'M'sieur Rohan will wish to know where I have brought you, *mademoiselle*,' Jacques said uncomfortably. 'He will not be pleased to know you are here, but I cannot lie to him.'

'Then tell him the truth,' Sabine said with bravado.

Jacques's brow became increasingly furrowed. 'He is a good man, *mademoiselle* — all the world would tell you so — but he has had to be strong — to bear everything on his shoulders. It has not been easy — and he does not like to be crossed.'

She thought, I knew that before I met him.

She shrugged, forcing a faint smile. 'I'll take my chance.' And paused. 'Before you go, can you tell me where I can get supplies? Without being disloyal to M'sieur Rohan, of course.'

There was a palpable hesitation, then he sighed. 'There is an Intermarché in Villereal, *mademoiselle*. Now goodbye — and good luck.'

He sounded convinced she would need it, Sabine thought as he trudged off. She looked up at the hill, but the château was invisible from this angle behind its enshrouding of trees. But it was there, just the same, like prying eyes peering round the corner of a thick curtain.

And he was there too. She was starkly aware of it. A man it was not wise to cross, whose angry scorn had already bruised her. And a man to whom she had just thrown down a deliberate challenge.

She said again, 'I'll take my chance,' and walked towards the archway.

CHAPTER THREE

SABINE didn't know what to expect. This had been her mother's house, after all, and Isabelle had left it over twenty-two years ago, and not been back since.

She was half anticipating having to fight her way through a jungle of undergrowth to reach the front door. But she was totally mistaken. A neat flagged area confronted her, flanked by the wall of some storage building on one side and the length of the house on the other. There were narrow flowerbeds in need of weeding on both sides, and in the sheltered corner between the store and the wall a tall rose lifted imperious petals like flames.

Beyond the store, the garden opened out into an untidy sloping lawn, with trees and shrubs, and the flags narrowed to a terrace. Sabine saw that the arched motif had been repeated in the french windows all the way along the front of the house and the stout wooden entrance. The rooms seemed bare, she thought, peering in through the dusty panes. Directly in front of the door was a small ornamental pool, with a fountain, although, naturally, it wasn't playing at the moment.

Once again Sabine had the curious sensation that time had stopped and run back.

But she was just being over-imaginative, she chided herself. Some kind soul had just been keeping the garden under reasonable control — that was all.

She tried the key in the lock. To her surprise, it turned easily, and she stepped inside. She found herself in a large square hall, with a pair of half-glazed doors ahead of her leading directly into the kitchen, and wooden double doors to her left, giving access to the rest of the house.

She tried these first. The room she entered ran the width of the house, with windows at both ends. She opened them and threw back the shutters, letting light flood in. The floor was tiled in a deep terracotta shade, but there was no furniture apart from a black enamelled stove standing in one corner on a raised hearth.

There were two doors in the far wall, and she opened each in turn. One was bare, but the other contained a range of old-fashioned fitted wardrobes, and a vast wooden bedstead, the head and footboards elaborately carved.

Sabine stared round her. The house smelt damp, of course, and there was a thin layer of dust everywhere, but there was none of the squalor and decay she had feared.

She went into the kitchen. A big scrubbed table stood in the middle of the room, and a vast dresser almost filled one wall. There was an old-fashioned sink under the window, and a new-looking electric cooker, with cupboards on both sides. A stable-type door led to the rear garden.

A further door led off to the right, with a tiled passage taking her to the bathroom, and another large square room at the end, which was probably the diningroom. From this a spiral staircase led upwards to a similar-sized room with windows on all sides, and

Sabine realised she must be in the tower she'd noticed on the way in.

The tower and the rose, she thought as she descended cautiously. I can't seem to get away from them.

She went slowly back to the kitchen. Only two sounds disturbed the silence — a fly buzzing desultorily against the window, and a tap dripping into the sink.

Well, at least that meant the water was turned on. She tried the light switch by the door, and discovered there was power too. That was odd, she thought, when the house was unoccupied. But it made it habitable, for which she was grateful. She would have hated it if she had to admit defeat, and crawl off to a hotel somewhere. She'd included a sleeping-bag in the luggage she'd brought with her, so she could manage.

She unloaded the car and carried everything in, dumping it all in the middle of the *salon*. Then she retrieved her map, plotted the route to Villereal, and made a list of what she wanted to buy.

Villereal was charming, and busy too, with its narrow streets and central square with a timbered-covered market. But exploration would have to wait. She had more pressing matters in hand. And the supermarket Jacques had mentioned was sited on the outskirts of town, she discovered.

Cleaning materials were the first priority, and enough china, cutlery and glassware for her own use. It was doubtful, she told herself wryly, whether she would be doing any entertaining.

After that, she could have fun. She wandered round the aisles, filling up her trolley with cheese, sliced ham and wedges of terrine, lingering over the huge butchery section, where the cuts of meat looked so different from those she was used to.

Finally she chose a plump boiling fowl, in deference to that great Gascon King of France, Henri Quatre, whose ambition it had been to see that all his subjects were well fed enough to have a chicken in their pot each week, and had made *La Poule Au Pot* a loved and traditional name for restaurants. Perhaps, she thought, her *poule au pot,* made as Maman had taught her, would make her feel less of an alien.

Her choice made, she went back for vegetables to accompany it, recklessly adding a demi-kilo of the huge firm-fleshed tomatoes, as well as nectarines, oranges and a punnet of strawberries to her collection. Her last purchase should have been bread — she picked a flat circular loaf rather than a baguette — but she succumbed to temptation and bought one of the plastic containers of the local *vin ordinaire,* amazingly cheap and good for its price, and several bottles of water too.

Driving back to the house through the small backroads was more difficult than she'd anticipated, and she took a couple of wrong turnings. She could have cried with relief when at last she passed the war memorial with the crucifix and realised the next track led to the farm.

And the house no longer seemed to be on the defensive, she realised as she parked the car. The late afternoon sun lent a warmer, more welcoming glow to its washed stones, and that exterior wall wasn't a barrier, but a promise of security. She thought, I've come home.

It took several journeys to unload her provisions from the boot. She put everything away in the kitchen cupboards, then went out to lock the car. It was probably unnecessary, she thought, but old habits died hard.

Then she saw him.

In fact, it was impossible to miss him. He was standing in the archway, hands on hips. Sabine halted, her hands balling into fists at her sides.

'What do you want?' Her voice rang with defiance.

'That's what I came to ask you.' He strolled forward, and Sabine fought down a prickle of apprehension.

'That's close enough,' she said sharply.

His brows rose mockingly. 'Do I make you nervous?'

'You make me angry.'

'And you,' he said, 'make me curious. Tell me, Mademoiselle Riquard, what possessed you to come here?'

'My name is Russell,' she said tightly. 'And my reasons are my own affair.'

'Russell,' he repeated slowly. 'So, Isabelle found another fool to marry her in England. Your French is excellent, but that is where you come from — isn't it?'

'I'm not ashamed of it,' she retorted, taut with anger over his reference to her mother. 'Anyway, we're all Europeans now — aren't we?' she mimicked his own phrasing.

'And that's why you've come — for international reasons?' His tone was openly derisive. 'I ask your pardon. I thought there might be some — personal motive.'

Sabine shrugged. 'I admit I was — curious too.'

'And has your curiosity been satisfied?'

'Not by any means,' she returned crisply.

He said quietly, 'I am sorry to hear that.' There was a pause. Then, 'How much would it cost, *mademoiselle*, to buy that satisfaction?'

The heat of the windless afternoon lay on her like a blanket, but suddenly she felt deathly cold. She said huskily, 'I — don't understand.'

'It is quite simple. I would like you to leave, preferably today, but by tomorrow at the latest. And I am willing to pay whatever price you ask — within reason.'

She gave a small uneven laugh. 'Just like that? You must be completely mad.'

'I am altogether sane, I assure you. And I hope you'll give my offer serious consideration.'

'It's not worth considering,' she said. 'It's an insult.'

'You don't yet know how much I am prepared to offer.' He looked at her grimly. 'Your presence here, *mademoiselle*, is intolerable. Surely you can see that.'

'I see nothing of the kind, and I'll leave when I'm ready,' Sabine said grittily. She shrugged, feigning nonchalance. 'Anyway, I may decide to stay. I'm a freelance. I can work anywhere, especially now.'

'If this is a ploy to force up the price, you'll be disappointed,' he said harshly. 'Contrary to what your mother may have told you, the de Rochefort family is no longer a well from which you can draw money like water.'

'My mother never mentioned anything about your family,' she denied hotly. 'And, having met some of you now, I can't honestly say I blame her. I'd have wanted to wipe you out — forget all about you, too.'

She paused. 'And, for the record, I wouldn't touch one *centime* of your rotten money.'

He shrugged. 'Then I will have to try other methods.'

She stared at him. 'What do you propose to do? Evict me from my mother's house? You have no right.'

'Legally, perhaps no,' he said softly. 'But the moral grounds are a different matter. Your mother, *mademoiselle*, left a trail of devastation behind her when she departed from our lives. I was only a boy of ten at the time, but it left its mark on me too. I do not propose to allow this to happen a second time — with you.'

'You can do exactly as you please,' she said thickly. 'But I will not listen to any more of your rotten insinuations about my mother. I loved her, and when she died I felt as if every light in the world had dimmed.'

For a moment, he was granite-still. The he said icily, 'You were not alone in that. My stepfather, whom I loved dearly also, had a complete breakdown when she left — when she abandoned him as she did.' His face was bleak. 'Presumably she never told you that either? No, I thought not.' He shook his head. 'If she never spoke of us, *mademoiselle*, believe me, it was through shame.'

'I've heard enough,' Sabine flung at him. 'If Maman ran away, it was because she had good and sufficient reason.' She took a deep breath. 'You ordered me off your land a few hours ago. Now I'm telling you to go, and don't come back. I am not for sale, not now, not ever.'

He took a step towards her, and she bent swiftly and snatched up a stone from the flowerbed beside her.

'Go.' Her voice rose. 'I said get out of here.'

He raked her from head to foot with one long, contemptuous look, then turned on his heel, and strode away under the arch and out of sight.

The tension drained from her, and she sagged limply against the front doorpost. She realised she was still gripping the stone, and dropped it with a little horrified cry. What the hell had she thought she was going to do with it — throw it at him?

She couldn't have. She wasn't violent — or hysterical. She'd never behaved in her life as she'd just done, and she couldn't understand or justify her reactions.

She wasn't a total dummy where men were concerned. She was reasonably attractive, and outgoing, and normally she had little difficulty in establishing cordial relationships in both her working and social life. She'd always had boyfriends, although so far she hadn't been tempted to engage in any serious commitment. Casual encounters that ended in bed had never been her scene, and in today's sexual climate they were not simply tacky, but positively dangerous.

Usually, she met people halfway, and tried not to make snap judgements about them. She hoped they would make the same allowances for her.

But this man — this arrogant de Rochefort creature — galled her as no one had ever done before. It wasn't just the terrible things he'd implied about Isabelle, although, God knew, they were bad enough. It was his totally unwarranted attitude to herself.

He seemed to have hated her on sight, yet he knew nothing about her, except that she bore a passing physical resemblance to Isabelle. And on such flimsy grounds she'd apparently been tried and sentenced. It was just assumed that she had some ulterior motive in coming here, and she wasn't allowed to defend herself. The injustice of it numbed her.

The worst her mother could be charged with was running away. And was it any wonder she'd fled, if she'd been subjected to the same bullying and threats by an earlier generation of de Rocheforts? Sabine thought hotly. That—arrogant brute had implied that her mother had taken his family for a ride financially, yet, according to Ruth Russell, Isabelle had been pregnant and penniless, reduced to working as a mother's help when Hugh met her. The two stories contradicted each other.

She looked up at the cloudless sky. She said out loud, 'I'm going to find out exactly what transpired all those years ago, and I'm not leaving here until I know the truth. I'm going to clear my mother's name, and the great M'sieur Rohan——' she almost spat the name '—is going to eat every last insulting word.'

She went back into the house and slammed the door.

She felt too uptight to embark on cooking her chicken dish that night, so she organised a simpler meal of terrine, followed by an omelette and fruit.

A search of the outside store revealed two folding canvas garden chairs, dilapidated but useable. She carried them on to the terrace in front of the house, and sat down, intending to read one of the paperback books she'd brought with her until the light faded.

But concentration on the story was well-nigh impossible. Every time she heard the slightest noise, she found herself glancing towards the archway.

Stop being stupid, she adjured herself, annoyed by her own twitchiness. He won't come back. He wouldn't dare.

She paused, grimacing. Did she really believe that?

He was the kind of man who looked capable of anything—who lived life entirely on his own terms. Physically, he wasn't her type at all, she thought, subjecting him to a critical mental review. Some women might find him attractive, but she didn't go for loose-limbed, olive-skinned men whose black hair flopped across their foreheads. Besides which, his nose was too long, his eyes were too heavy-lidded, and his chin too damned assertive by half. And his firm mouth, when it wasn't compressed by anger, had a disturbingly sensual curve, which made her skin prickle even to recall it.

Would he make love, perhaps, as fiercely as he hated? she wondered, then stopped right there, giving herself a mental shake. That was one line of conjecture she certainly didn't need to pursue.

But he would not, she admitted reluctantly, be easy to forget. Dangerous, she thought, and ruthless too. Master of all he surveyed, and used to his own way. Well, he'd come unstuck this time. She couldn't be bought and she wouldn't be forced out of here.

She realised she was revolving everything they'd said to each other round and round in her mind. That brief reference to his stepfather was haunting her, and she wished she'd found out more while she had the chance.

Perhaps it had been a mistake to dismiss him so summarily after all, she thought with dissatisfaction.

The little he'd said indicated that his stepfather had been deeply emotionally involved with Isabelle. If so, it was more than probable that he was the father of her baby.

My father, Sabine thought. Which would make this Rohan some kind of relation, legally if not by blood.

The thought made her shudder, but the fact that he hadn't referred to the ghastly possibility himself made her wonder if Isabelle had kept her pregnancy a secret from the de Rochefort clan. But why should she do such a thing — an unmarried girl who would desperately need help and support — especially fron her child's father?

It made no sense at all, but she was too tired and emotionally battered herself to rationalise about it any more. She would get some rest, and face the whole problem in the morning.

Her sleeping-bag looked forlorn in the middle of that vast bed. She shed her clothes, and slipped quickly into its impersonal embrace. But, weary though she was, sleep remained elusive at first.

Her thoughts kept returning obsessively to the Château La Tour Monchauzet, and its master. They might be hidden behind their curtain of trees, but she felt oppressed by their proximity just the same, as if they were standing guard over her.

'The picture on the card was deceptive, she thought drowsily. It showed a fairy-tale palace, but in reality it was Bluebeard's Castle.

And when at last she fell asleep it was to find herself

in the château, running endlessly through a labyrinth of rooms, searching for something that was always just beyond her reach. While, behind her, on silent feet, a dark man with hooded eyes stalked her. And waited.

She woke with a headache, but then nightmares always had that effect on her, she thought moodily, as she showered, and put on shorts and a sleeveless top.

She cut a wedge from the loaf, spread it with cherry jam, and carried it, with a mug of coffee, on to the terrace. The air was cool, the grass was damp with dew, and there was a faint mist hanging over the nearby fields. All in all, it promised to be another heavenly day, she thought, feeling her spirits rise almost perceptibly. And no nasty dream was going to spoil it for her.

A small brown lizard scuttled across the flags, and paused for a moment, at a safe distance, flanks heaving gently.

'Well, good morning to you too,' Sabine said, as it dashed up the wall in a blur of movement, and vanished into the eaves. So she wasn't the sole occupant after all, she thought, amused.

So far, she'd done the absolute minimum necessary to allow herself to camp in the house overnight. But today it was going to be different. Today, she was going to do some heavy-duty cleaning — stamp her seal on the place, and make it her own.

If she was going to stay for any length of time, she was going to need some furniture at least, she thought frowningly. A chest of drawers for her clothes, for instance. A comfortable chair, or maybe a bean-bag

for the *salon*. And proper bedding. She wasn't used to
being without a pillow.

As she turned to go back inside, she saw something
white lying on the hall floor. An envelope, she realised,
as she bent to retrieve it. She hadn't merely failed to
notice it on her way out. She'd trodden on it. Her
footprint was stencilled across the thick hand-made
paper.

It must be a mistake, she thought, turning it over in
her hands, and noting there was no superscription. No
stamp either, so it had been delivered by hand, either
last night when she was asleep, or very early this
morning.

She thought, I don't really want to open this. At the
same time, she knew she would have to.

It contained a single sheet of paper. The handwritten
message was brief and formal. The Baronne de
Rochefort presented her compliments to Mademoiselle
Russell, and would be obliged if she would call at the
château at three o'clock that afternoon.

A royal summons, no less, Sabine thought drily.
Madame Héloise seemed to have recovered from her
shock and the accident, and be back in fighting form
again.

And she had all morning and part of the afternoon
to decide whether or not to accept this imperious
invitation. At the moment she felt totally disinclined to
do any such thing.

I'll consider it while I work, she thought, stuffing the
letter into her shorts pocket. She started in the kitchen.
Yesterday, she'd given just the cupboards she needed
to use a superficial wipe-over. This time, every drawer,

every shelf and every surface was cleaned to within an inch of its life, and the tiled floor scrubbed till it shone. Feeling thoroughly ill-tempered gave one energy, she thought, as she started on the dust and cobwebs in the *salon*.

She stopped at noon for some bread and cheese, and a glass of wine diluted with water, then plunged doggedly back into housework.

She was absorbed in cleaning the arched windows when she heard the sound of a car engine. Every muscle tensed, and she swallowed nervously, but she carried on with her appointed task with renewed concentration. She would not — she would not look round, she vowed.

A girl's pleasant voice behind her said, 'Mademoiselle Russell?'

Sabine turned in swift astonishment. The newcomer was about her own age, on the plump side of curvaceous, chestnut-haired and pretty. She was also smiling broadly, and offering to shake hands, which must count as some kind of first, Sabine thought as she hastily wiped her own hand on her shorts.

She said doubtfully, 'Should I know you?'

The girl laughed and shook her head. 'I live at the farm with my aunt, so we're your neighbours. My name is Marie-Christine Lavaux.'

'Oh.' So this was a social call, Sabine thought, relaxing. 'May I offer you something — coffee — a glass of wine?'

'At any other time it would be a pleasure.' Marie-Christine wrinkled her nose in a small comic grimace. 'But unfortunately, *mademoiselle,* I have been sent to escort you to your appointment at the château.' She paused. 'Among other duties, I am Madame de Rochefort's secretary. You found the letter I left this morning, I hope?'

'Oh, yes, I found it,' Sabine said, her voice flattening in disappointment. 'But I'm not sure I wish to comply with the *Baronne*'s request.'

Marie-Christine's brows shot up. 'Is there some problem?'

'You tell me,' Sabine returned. 'The last time I saw the lady, she was almost unconscious.'

Marie-Christine grimaced again. 'Ah, the accident. Well, she is fully restored to health today. *Madame* is stronger than she looks.'

She would need to be, Sabine thought. Aloud, she said, 'Do you know why she wishes to see me?'

'I am only a secretary at the château. *Madame* does not confide in me to that extent.' Marie-Christine shrugged. 'Presumably she wishes to thank you for assisting her yesterday, after her accident.' She gave Sabine a pleading smile. 'Why not come with me, and see?' She paused. 'You may wish to change first, perhaps,' she suggested diplomatically.

'And perhaps not,' Sabine said levelly. 'I'm cool and comfortable as I am. And this appointment was not my idea.'

Marie-Christine gave her a wry look. 'That is exactly why I was sent to fetch you. And I shall be in big trouble if I return alone. *Madame* expects her wishes to be obeyed.'

'She's not the only one,' Sabine muttered.

'*Pardon*?'

'It doesn't matter,' Sabine said resignedly. 'All right, then. I give in. But I hope *Madame* doesn't expect me in a hat and gloves.'

She compromised with one of the few dresses she'd brought with her—a simple navy cotton in a button-through style, with short sleeves, a deep square neck and a full skirt.

Then, obeying an impulse she barely understood, she took the silver medallion out of the inner pocket of her bag, where she'd zipped it for safekeeping, and fastened the chain round her neck.

A talisman, she thought. For protection. Which I may need.

She drew a deep breath, then went out to keep her appointment.

CHAPTER FOUR

As SABINE emerged from the bedroom, she found Marie-Christine standing in the empty *salon*, staring round her.

'The furnishings are a bit sparse at the moment,' Sabine said lightly. 'I hope to go shopping tomorrow.'

'But there is no need,' Marie-Christine protested. 'There is plenty of furniture belonging to the house. After M'sieur Fabien died, my aunt arranged for it to be stored, because a house that is left empty can sometimes attract thieves, you understand. She's been in Paris on business for two days, but she'll be back this evening, so you can speak to her about it.'

Sabine was totally lost. 'Who was Monsieur Fabien?' she enquired, as they went out to the car.

Marie-Christine's lively face sobered. 'He was the *Baron's* brother — his twin, but younger by just a half-hour, and so different — in looks, temperament — everything. He was the true *vigneron*,' she added, sighing. 'He loved the land, and understood the grape.' She paused. 'Monsieur Gaston concerned himself with other things.'

'Monsieur Gaston being the *Baron*, I take it.' Sabine also hesitated for a moment. 'So, where does — Monsieur Rohan ——' she stumbled over the name a little ' — fit in?'

'Monsieur Fabien married a Madame Saint Yves,

who was a widow with a little boy,' Marie-Christine explained readily. 'She was having another baby, but something went wrong—apparently, she was never strong—and she and the child both died.' She shook her head. 'It was a terrible thing—a great tragedy. Monsieur Rohan stayed with Monsieur Fabien and was brought up as his own son—at first anyway.'

Sabine stared ahead of her through the windscreen. Fabien de Rochefort, she thought. Rohan's stepfather, who had loved and lost her mother, had a name, if not a face.

Maybe I know now who my real father was, she thought. But the swift excitement bubbling inside her was mingled inevitably with sadness, because it was all too late. He was lost to her too.

She asked colourlessly, 'When did Monsieur Fabien die? How long ago?'

Marie-Christine considered. 'It must be over a year and a half—nearly two years. Time goes so fast,' she added apologetically.

'Why was the house only emptied then?'

'Because he had been living there.'

'Even though the house belonged to my mother?' Sabine queried, her heart thumping. She tried to sound casual. 'I suppose he was some kind of tenant.'

'My aunt will be able to explain better, perhaps.' Marie-Christine was clearly embarrassed. 'It is none of my affair and, besides, it was all a long time ago.'

'I'm sorry to ask so many questions,' Sabine said, after another pause. 'But apart from the fact that my mother obviously lived here at some time I know nothing at all.'

Marie-Christine bit her lip as they turned on to the road leading up to the château. 'Well, I wish I could be more help, but all I've heard are rumours—a lot of confused stories. It wouldn't be fair to repeat them,' she added firmly.

'I suppose not,' Sabine said wistfully. She paused again, then tried a new tack. 'So, apart from the *Baron* and Madame de Rochefort, who else lives at the château?'

'Well, Rohan lives there—for the time being, anyway. And Antoinette, of course.'

'Oh.' Sabine digested that. 'Is—is she—Rohan's wife?'

Marie-Christine laughed. 'Not yet, but it is expected. It would be a very suitable marriage. She's Madame Héloise's niece, and very beautiful. Her parents were killed in an accident when she was very young, and she has been brought up at the château, almost as the daughter of the house. The *Baron* and his wife have no children of their own,' she added.

'I see,' was all Sabine could think of in reply.

She never forgot her first proper view of the château. It was much smaller than she'd imagined, just a country house, she thought, which had been added to in a haphazard way over the centuries. The stones glowed like warm apricots in the afternoon sun, and the jumble of towers and turrets with their high pointed roofs topped with blue-grey tiles had an endearing and slightly eccentric charm.

Sabine had half expected to be taken round to some tradesman's entrance, but Marie-Christine led the way to the main door, chattering nineteen to the dozen, clearly relieved that her mission was almost accomplished. She was probably glad that the inquisition was over too, Sabine thought drily.

Some parts of the house had been closed off, for economic reasons, she was told. Madame de Rochefort and Antoinette both had suites on the first floor, while the *Baron* occupied rooms at ground level. She didn't volunteer any information about where Rohan Saint Yves slept.

One of the main rooms, and the most beautiful, the grand chamber, was used solely for vineyard business these days. All the entertaining was done there, and there were regular wine-tastings for customers.

'May I see it?' Sabine asked.

'Another day, perhaps,' Marie-Christine said noncommittally. 'We must not keep *Madame* waiting.'

After the radiance of the sunlit walls, the interior of the château was frankly a disappointment. The entrance hall, although large and square, was panelled in some dark wood, which made it gloomy, and the ancestral portraits which stared disapprovingly down on Sabine as she mounted the stairs did nothing to lighten the atmosphere.

To reach Madame de Rochefort's suite, they had to traverse a series of other rooms, most of them shuttered to exclude the sun. The furniture seemed very grand, and totally impersonal, as if the rooms were never used, except as a passage to somewhere else. Sabine couldn't imagine anyone lounging in those chairs, or throwing a book or a magazine down on one of the tables.

This place is like a labyrinth, she thought with a

sudden shiver, as yet another door opened in front of her. Just like last night's bad dream. She had the sensation that if she looked over her shoulder she would find Rohan Saint Yves watching her from the shadows. . . Her hand lifted and touched the medallion at her breast, as if warding off an evil spirit.

They stepped out into a corridor, richly carpeted in Turkey red.

'This is *madame's* part of the house.' Marie-Christine lowered her voice. 'She has carpet everywhere because she said the noise of the servants' shoes on the polished floors made her head ache.' She rolled her eyes, then sobered, tapping respectfully on the double doors at the end of the passage.

'Come in.' The answering voice was clear, controlled and authoritative, giving no sign of yesterday's weakness.

Marie-Christine turned her friendly grin on Sabine. '*Courage*,' she whispered. 'You're on your own now.' And pushed her gently but firmly into the room.

The royal summons had clearly brought Sabine to the throne room of the palace, she thought drily, as she halted inside the door. The far end of the room was built on a higher level than the rest, and was reached by a single step. And there, seated by a window in a big winged chair, shaded by peach silk curtains, was Héloïse de Rochefort.

She was not a tall woman, but the classic smoothness of her grey hair, immaculately dressed, gave her an air of distinction. To Sabine, used to Aunt Ruth's dab of power and smudge of lipstick, the *Baronne's maquillage* made her appear as if she was wearing an exquisite but remote mask, spoiled only by the small piece of sticking plaster on her forehead. Her eyes were deep-set and cold, and her dress in matching blue emphasised an impression of chilly reserve. She wore an antique brooch on one shoulder, and her hands, discreetly beringed, were folded in her lap, and one wrist had been bandaged.

'Miss Russell,' she said almost musingly in English. 'Please take a seat.' She indicated a brocaded chair placed opposite to hers, and at an angle.

Sabine obeyed, folding her hands in her lap with equal composure. She had the oddest impression that she was taking part in a play, for which she knew neither her lines, nor the stage directions.

Madame turned her head slightly. 'Antoinette, my dear, you haven't met this young lady, who is paying a short visit from England.'

When the leading lady's on stage, you don't notice the rest of the cast, Sabine thought wryly, the wording of *madame's* introduction not lost on her, as a young woman got up from a sofa in another part of the room, and came forward with open reluctance.

She was taller than Sabine, and older too. Her thick dark hair fell in a waving mass to her shoulders, and she had a short, straight nose, a mouth that was full-lipped to the point of petulance, and almond-shaped brown eyes, currently studying Sabine without friendliness. She wore a pale yellow dress cut to emphasise shapely legs and the thrust of her rounded breasts. Altogether, she had the kind of gloss normally associated with models and film stars, and it seemed oddly out of place here in her aunt's elegant sitting-room.

Her fingers barely touched Sabine's in greeting, but one swift head-to-toe appraisal absorbed everything she had on, and dismissed it. The de Rochefort clan, as a whole, had a pretty strong line in contempt, Sabine decided, not letting her own polite smile slip by one iota.

So, this was the girl Rohan Saint Yves was planning to marry. His scowl wedded to her sulks, eh? Well, they were welcome to each other.

Antoinette turned and addressed the older woman in her own language. 'Tante Héloise — is it really necessary that we do this — that we receive this person?'

'Entirely necessary,' Madame returned imperturbably. 'And I should warn you, Antoinette, that Miss Russell understands our language perfectly — and speaks it too.'

She didn't need to be warned, Sabine thought drily, as Antoinette flushed angrily.

'Now ring the bell, *ma chère*, for Ernestine to bring us some tea, then you may leave us. I wish to speak privately with Miss Russell.' She smiled. 'But how can I be so formal with Isabelle's child? What is your name, my dear?'

'Sabine, *madame*.'

She saw the upright figure stiffen suddenly, and the hands clench together in her lap.

Then, 'What insolence!' Antoinette exclaimed shrilly. 'That is a de Rochefort family name. She had no right.' Her intervention snapped the sudden tension in the room, as if a wire had been cut.

The *Baronne's* rose-tinted lips twisted slightly. 'Calm yourself, my child. We do not have a monopoly in names—or very much else these days,' she added, almost as an aside. 'And Sabine has not been used as a de Rochefort name for several generations. Now ring for tea, as I requested you, please.'

Antoinette looked mutinous, but she obeyed, leaving the room with something of a flounce.

'So,' Madame de Rochefort said, when they were alone. 'Now we can talk comfortably.'

Can we? Sabine wondered. She said levelly, 'I hope you've recovered from your unfortunate accident, *madame*.'

The *Baronne* gave a silvery laugh. 'Oh, do not remind me of my own stupidity, I beg you. I am so ashamed. But for a moment, you understand, I thought I had seen a ghost.' She nodded slowly. 'Yes, you are Isabelle's daughter without mistake.'

'Is that the reason you invited me here—to a house where I'm clearly not welcome—to have another look at me?'

'No, of course not,' the *Baronne* returned peevishly. 'I wished to express my regrets for my nephew's— hasty reaction. Such a dear boy. So devoted to our family's interests.'

She paused. 'I was sorry to hear that your mother is dead.'

'Thank you,' Sabine said quietly.

'Tell me—was she content in England? Your father—was he a good husband to her?'

'They—seemed very happy,' Sabine returned neutrally.

'She grew up here, of course. Her father, Hercule, was our *maître de chai,* responsible for making our wine, as Rohan is now. But no doubt she told you this?'

'No, *madame*.' Sabine shook her head. 'My mother never mentioned her life here, except to say that I had no grandparents.'

'She said nothing else?' *Madame's* fingers twisted the magnificent ruby she wore. 'But that is — quite extraordinary.'

'I thought so too,' Sabine agreed. 'No doubt she had her reasons,' she added pointedly.

'Ah.' *Madame's* eyes seemed to look past her into a different time. 'She was very lovely. My mother-in-law was alive then, and she indulged her — encouraged her artistic talents, I believe.'

She sighed faintly. 'An exquisite child, growing into a beautiful girl. Unfortunately, she was also one of those women born to be adored by men. That can often bring more grief than pleasure, don't you find?'

'It's not something that's ever concerned me particularly,' Sabine said drily. 'Are you saying that's why my mother ran away from here — because she was loved too much?'

'She was certainly worshipped by my brother-in-law Fabien,' the *Baronne* said flatly. 'He always did, it seems. But he was contracted to marry elsewhere — a suitable marriage, and Isabelle was a dangerous distraction.'

She paused. 'That was why, when she showed promise as an artist, my mother-in-law arranged for her to be trained in Paris — and even provided money for the purpose.' She sighed faintly. 'It was thought — everyone assumed — she would marry in her turn, and that would be the end of it. But she didn't. And when Hercule became ill she came back to look after him, and it all began again.

'By this time Fabien was a widower, you understand. After Hercule died, it was suggested that Isabelle should stay on for a while — assist with the children. Antoinette was just three.' Her face softened perceptibly. 'And so spirited. None of the nursemaids I had engaged were of any use at all. Rohan was older, of course, but he needed the kind of attention that Fabien could not give him, although he was devoted to the boy.'

She threw back her head. 'It was a terrible mistake, of course, for Isabelle to stay — to be close to Fabien again. I — realised that at once. But it was too late. He had already asked her to marry him. We protested, naturally, but he was adamant. He had married once for duty, he told my husband. This time he would make his own choice.'

'So they were actually engaged?' Sabine queried.

'Yes, but there were problems. Your mother had learned to be independent in Paris — her own woman. She refused outright to live here at the château. She wanted a house of her own, and she persuaded Fabien to give her the money to buy Les Hiboux in her own name. He could refuse her nothing, of course, and she bought the house. I suppose he thought that when they were married they would live there together.'

She was silent for a moment, then she said harshly, 'And then she left — disappeared — without a word — without a trace, only two weeks before the wedding.'

'So soon?'

The *Baronne* nodded. 'Fabien was not here when she went. He was on a business trip to California. She had — laid her plans carefully, it seems. He was inconsolable when he found what she'd done. It — destroyed him. Nothing was ever the same again.'

'But she couldn't just go, like that. She wasn't a cruel person.'

The *Baronne* shrugged. 'Clearly, she never loved him as he did her. I sensed that, but it is the same in many relationships. There is one who loves, and the other who allows that devotion.' She paused for a moment, biting her lip as if fighting for her composure.

Sabine was silent too. It was not easy to come to terms with this view of Isabelle as someone who received love without giving in return. That wasn't the woman she remembered at all. But the memory of Hugh Russell's blind, unthinking adoration of her mother raised doubts in her mind.

I was a child after all, she thought. I saw only what I wanted to. Isabelle's acquisition of Les Hiboux seemed inexplicable too. It was an oddly cold-blooded act to coax a large sum of money from someone she had no intention of marrying to buy a house she didn't intend to live in.

And why had she secretly kept it all those years, when she didn't want it? Why hadn't she arranged for the house to be sold so that Fabien de Rochefort could at least be repaid to some extent?

Because she didn't want to be traced, that was why, she thought. And negotiations over the sale of a house — signature of the various contracts would have inevitably revealed her whereabouts.

But surely even having second thoughts about marriage wasn't enough to prompt that kind of reaction, particularly as Isabelle must have known she was expecting Fabien's child. Yet she'd been prepared to chance it, alone and pregnant as she was.

Something must have happened, Sabine told herself. Some traumatic, terrible thing. And I have to know what that was. I can't just leave it and walk away. She said quietly, 'If you want me to explain why my mother acted as she did, *madame,* I can't. I only recently discovered her connection with this place, and that was by accident. She — left some things.' She took the wine label from the envelope, and handed it across. 'This was among them, and that's why I came here.'

The *Baronne* had retreated behind her mask again, but her lips tightened as she glanced at the label.

'It was one she designed for our château at Fabien's request. A new label, he said, to mark a new beginning for the *vignoble.* He — insisted that it be used, even afterwards. The legend of the tower and the rose,' she added, half to herself.

'And there was also this.' Sabine unfastened the chain round her neck, and put the medallion gently into the *Baronne's* hand. 'It obviously belonged to your family, and I'd like to return it.'

The older woman was very still, staring down at it. 'Where did you get this?'

'I found it. It must have been another gift.'

'Yes.' *Madame* drew a deep breath like a sigh. 'Another gift.' She opened a small drawer in the pretty rosewood table beside her chair, dropped the trinket into it, then closed it with a kind of finality.

Then she looked at Sabine. 'Why have you come here, Miss Russell? Fabien is dead — your mother also. Why do you want to probe into old wounds like this? What do you hope to gain?'

Sabine lifted her chin. 'I want the truth,' she said. 'It's that simple.'

The *Baronne* shrugged. 'The truth? Your mother was a silly greedy girl — a gold-digger who wanted to marry above her station, but took fright at the last moment, without caring what hurt she bestowed. That is the truth.'

'I'm sorry,' Sabine said. 'But I don't believe it.'

The *Baronne* leaned forward, her eyes fixed piercingly on Sabine's face. 'Be advised by me, Miss Russell. Take a little tour in our beautiful country — sit in the sunshine — drink some wine. But ask no more questions. Enough harm has been done.'

She looked past Sabine. 'And here comes our tea,' she added, her face softening into an approach to warmth. 'It is good of you to save Ernestine the trouble of the stairs, *mon cher*. As you see, I am entertaining a visitor.'

Sabine sat rigidly upright in her chair. She didn't have to look round to know who'd entered the room. Every sense, every nerve-ending in her body was tingling with sudden awareness.

'So I was informed,' Rohan Saint Yves said grimly, as he set down the tray. 'Ernestine, however, failed to tell me the identity of the guest. What are you doing here, *mademoiselle*?'

'How fierce you are, my dear Rohan,' the *Baronne* intervened, openly amused. 'I invited her, of course.'

'And I've clearly outstayed my welcome,' Sabine said tightly, rising from her chair.

Madame waved an imperious hand. 'No, no, sit down again, and we will all have tea together. Such a pleasant English custom,' she added as Sabine reluctantly subsided. 'Miss Russell and I have been talking over the past.'

Rohan drew up a chair with gilded legs which looked altogether too fragile for his tall frame.

'It's time that was forgotten in this house,' he said brusquely. 'We've dwelt too much on disaster — and former triumphs too. Now we should be occupied totally with the future, or we shall risk being left behind.'

'I gather you've been visiting Monsieur Jerome,' *Madame* remarked with a slight edge to her voice. 'I hope you found him well?'

Rohan shrugged. 'He's getting impatient,' he returned, enigmatically.

The *Baronne's* gathering frown dispersed almost magically as she espied a flat be-ribboned box on the tray. 'Macaroons from Saint Emilion!' she exclaimed. 'My favourites, you dear boy.' She turned to Sabine. 'These are the best macaroons in the world, *mademoiselle,* made from a centuries-old secret recipe. There is nothing like them. You must try some.' She paused. 'You have heard of Saint Emilion, of course.'

Sabine nodded. 'I passed it on the way here from Bordeaux. But I only associated it with wine.'

'It is a charming village — almost a temple to wine.' *Madame* filled her cup. 'I hope you have time to visit it before you leave. Cream or lemon, Miss Russell?'

'Lemon, please.' Sabine paused too. 'And I have all the time I need, *madame*,' she added with cool emphasis. Make what you want of that, she thought, flicking a glance under her lashes at the silent man lounging opposite her.

'Speaking of wine,' the *Baronne* said, as they sampled the macaroons, which Sabine found to be crisp on the outside, moist on the inside, with a delicate, delicious flavour. 'Have you tried our own Château La Tour Monchauzet? Because you must. As the granddaughter of a great *maître de chai,* your opinion would be valued.'

'I doubt that,' Sabine said drily. 'I'm no expert.'

'We are perhaps a little unusual in this region in that we produce only red wine,' the *Baronne* went on. 'Many of our neighbours in the Bergerac *vignoble* produce white wine, and often rosé too.'

'Which gives them immediately a greater share of the market,' Rohan put in drily. 'Our wine has been good, but it is not and never will be one of the great classic vintages of, say, the Bordeaux region. We should diversify too, and invest, if we wish to survive. Or we may live to see the vines ploughed up and turned into orchards as has been happening in other areas.'

'It is your uncle Gaston you have to convince, *mon cher,* not me,' the *Baronne* said with a shrug.

'As I am already aware,' Rohan replied with a certain curtness. 'At the moment, it seems impossible to convince him that any kind of action at all is necessary.'

'Quite impossible this afternoon, at any rate,' said the *Baronne.* 'Leon has taken him to Domme.'

Sabine cleared her throat. She had no wish to be drawn even marginally into any of the other de Rochefort family contentions. 'It's really time I was going, *madame*. Thank you for the tea.'

'It has been my pleasure — Sabine.' The mouth smiled but the blue eyes were oddly expressionless as the *Baronne* offered her hand. 'Rohan — make sure that Miss Russell samples some of our wine before she leaves. It may be her only opportunity.'

Sabine groaned inwardly. 'Really, that isn't necessary——' she began.

'Ah, but I insist for Hercule's sake.' *Madame* cut short the protest. 'Rohan, send Ernestine to me, if you please. I wish to rest now.'

He kissed her hand, his swift glance concerned. 'You shouldn't disturb yourself like this. There was no need. Is your headache better?'

'Completely gone, I assure you. And I wished to make amends a little. We were not gracious yesterday — especially as this child came so far to find us. I have spent a most interesting afternoon.'

And I'm fascinated to have met you — Tante Héloïse. Walking to the door, Sabine wondered detachedly what the reaction would be if she voiced her unspoken thought aloud, but decided not to risk it.

On one of the occasional tables, as she passed, she noticed a large silver-framed photograph of two young men, presumably the *Baron* and his brother. Apart from their fair hair and strong features, there was little to label them as twins, she thought, wondering which was her father, and which her uncle.

It seemed crazy that she couldn't ask outright —

claim the relationship which was almost certainly hers. But in the circumstances it seemed better to remain silent, particularly with Rohan Saint Yves marching grimly at her shoulder like some gaoler.

When they were in the corridor, she said tartly, 'I can find my own way out. Or are you afraid I'll make off with the family jewels?'

'Madame de Rochefort wishes you to taste our wine. I don't usually ignore her commands,' Rohan returned coolly. 'Indulge her, please.'

Sabine suspected that the *Baronne* was already sufficiently indulged, but she allowed herself to be escorted to the grand chamber.

It was a large, imposing room as the name suggested, its walls hung with tapestries, and with a minstrel's gallery at one end. A long polished table stood in the centre, holding an assortment of bottles, and a tray of glasses. Sabine looked round her with eager curiosity, her gaze lingering on one large central tapestry. The tower and the rose again, she thought. But this time there was an added element — the tower had a window, from which a girl, with one of the steeple-like headdresses of the fifteenth century, seemed to be peering down.

'You know the legend of La Tour Monchauzet?' Rohan had noticed where her eyes were fixed.

'I feel as if I should,' she admitted. 'I think I may have heard it as a bedtime story when I was a small child.' She racked her brain, trying to remember once more. 'Wasn't there something about a princess locked up by her cruel father?' she hazarded.

'The real story is not so fairy-tale,' Rohan said drily.

'The girl wasn't a princess, just an unfaithful de Rochefort wife.' He paused. 'Her name was Sabine,' he added without expression.

'Oh, really?' Sabine's eyes narrowed, and he laughed suddenly, his whole face changing, bringing home to her the full force of his considerable attraction.

'Yes, really,' he said. 'She was the first Sabine. Her husband found her one day wearing a rose pinned to her gown that was not from his garden, and guessed it was a gift from her lover. He was mad with anger and jealousy, so he locked her in the tower, with only a spinning-wheel for company. There she would stay, he told her, without food or water, until she had spun enough thread to weave new hangings for their marriage bed.'

'Sounds like a life sentence,' Sabine commented.

'It could well have been,' Rohan agreed, deadpan. 'Spinning, of course, was not the lady's chief skill.'

'What happened?'

He shrugged. 'Her lover came seeking her, worried because he hadn't received any word or token from her. By this time, she was too weak from hunger and thirst to call to him from the window. But the rose he had given her was still miraculously blooming on the breast of her gown. So, with her last remaining strength, she pushed it through the bars, and it fluttered down to his feet.'

'And he rescued her, and they lived happily ever after,' Sabine guessed.

'That's one version, certainly,' he agreed. 'But another says that he didn't notice the rose and simply rode away.'

'So what became of the girl?'

'She starved to death. Her husband gave out she'd perished of some wasting disease, and duly married someone else, less beautiful but more docile, who gave him twelve children.'

Sabine grimaced. 'I prefer the happy ending.'

'I'm sure you do,' he said, after a pause. 'But real life is rarely so tidy. You have only to look back a generation.'

She bit her lip, refusing to be drawn. 'Is there really a tower still?'

'Yes, in the woods,' he said. 'But my uncle says it is structurally unsound, with a danger of falling masonry, so no one is allowed near it.'

'It's a pity he doesn't have it repaired instead,' Sabine said. 'As it's featured on the château label, the legend could be used to attract visitors, and sell more wine.'

'Most of our wine is exported, and our sales are satisfactory at the moment,' Rohan said curtly. 'And attracting visitors has not been a priority of the château for a very long time. Not since my uncle's accident, in fact.'

'I'm sorry,' she said. 'I didn't know — although the Maison du Vin in Bergerac did warn there were no tours of the vineyard because the *Baron* wasn't well.'

'The *Baron's* general health is excellent,' he corrected her. 'However, he damaged his spine over twenty years ago, after being thrown from his horse, and has been in a wheelchair ever since.' He paused. 'It has made him — over-sensitive to the presence of strangers, perhaps.'

Sabine swallowed. 'The de Rocheforts seem to have suffered a lot of misfortune.'

'Not the least being the fact that the line ends with my uncle. Even before his accident it seemed doubtful that my aunt would ever have a child of her own. Afterwards, it was impossible.'

'But they have Antoinette,' she ventured, remembering what Marie-Christine had told her.

'Indeed they have.' Face and voice gave nothing away. 'I'd hoped, too, they might have a little peace,' he added more pointedly.

In other words, without my disruptive influence, Sabine thought wryly, turning her attention to the minstrel's gallery. 'That's beautiful,' she remarked, rather too brightly. 'Is it still used?'

'On occasion — say, if we have a big wine-tasting for overseas buyers. Or when the château is *en fête*, on Tante Héloïse's birthday, for example. Even my uncle puts in one of his rare public appearances then.' He paused. 'The next time, I suppose, will be the wedding.'

So it's true, Sabine thought. He is going to marry Antoinette. She remembered the beautiful, sullen face and the sensual movement of the other girl's body in the yellow dress, and an odd pang assailed her, piercing her to the heart with its intensity.

She cleared her throat. 'Will — will the wedding be soon?'

He nodded, almost casually. 'In a few weeks.'

By which time, I'll be gone, she thought, then, fiercely, And I'm glad I'll be gone.

Because, it occurred to her with heart-stopping suddenness, the last thing in the world she wanted was to be around when Rohan Saint Yves married Antoinette — or anyone else.

CHAPTER FIVE

'Is SOMETHING the matter?' Rohan's voice seemed to reach Sabine from a great distance. 'You're very pale.'

'I'm fine.' She found a voice from somewhere. 'It's very hot today. I'm just not used to it yet. . .' She made herself smile. 'Maybe some wine will do me good.'

'Very well.'

Sabine watched as Rohan chose a bottle and poured some of its contents into a glass. 'Try this.' He held it out to her. 'It's the '89 vintage.'

She took it, thankful that her hand wasn't trembling noticeably. Her knees seemed to have turned to water, her mind still reeling under the impact of the devastating revelation which had just come to her.

It's not possible, she thought. It's complete madness. This is the first time he's even been remotely civil to me, for God's sake. . .

She pulled herself together with an effort, trying to remember what she'd been told about wine-tasting, holding the glass carefully by the stem, and sniffing delicately.

'*Bravo!*' Rohan said satirically. 'What does that tell you?'

'Not a lot,' she admitted.

'Well, at least you are honest about that,' he remarked, and, in spite of her new-found feelings,

Sabine was sorely tempted to throw the wine in his face. 'Now drink some, but don't swallow it at once. Hold it in your mouth and think about it.'

Sabine obeyed, wrinkling her brow in concentration.

'You look fierce.' He sounded almost amused. 'Is it that bad?'

'Not at all,' she said, swallowing.

'Can you still taste the wine?'

'Yes,' she said, rather doubtfully.

'Don't sound so worried,' he advised drily. 'It's a young wine, not really up to drinking yet. You're not supposed to experience a great deal.' He picked up another bottle. 'Taste this instead. It's the '86.' He handed her the glass. 'This time, look at the colour first.'

'It's beautiful,' Sabine said. 'Like the heart of a ruby.'

'Now the bouquet.'

Sabine complied and gasped. 'That's completely different. It's got a lovely rich, warm aroma.'

'Good,' Rohan approved, his tone faintly sardonic. 'Now drink.' He filled a glass for himself. 'I'll join you.' He was watching her closely. 'So—what do you think?'

'It's wonderful,' Sabine said, as she swallowed. 'It's got this incredible fruity taste, rather like blackcurrant. But my mouth feels very dry, almost furry.'

'That's the tannin from the Cabernet Sauvignon grape. We use a combination of that and the Merlot, which is much softer, and the Malbec. One of the problems we've had of late is the wine keeping too much tannin as it matures. With all wine, it's the force — the long-lasting flavour in the throat — which matters.'

'But it's not unpleasant,' Sabine said, taking another mouthful, and savouring it.

'Nevertheless it is not to all tastes. Sometimes it can be caused by the age of the oak casks the wine is stored in. Some *vignerons* will tell you that a cask lasts only for four years. Ours have needed replacing for some time,' he added with a touch of grimness.

'If they're oak, they must be expensive.'

'They're not cheap,' he agreed. 'But a good vintage requires the best of care. I intend to see that it gets it.'

'Another customer for our wine, Rohan? No one told me.' At the sound of the voice from the doorway, they both swung round.

Gaston de Rochefort would always be a handsome man, in spite of his disability, but pain had carved deep and bitter lines across his forehead, and beside his mouth. The fair hair had faded to a dusty grey, and his skin looked pale and unhealthy, as if he spent too much time indoors, but the green eyes were lusty with life and rebellion against the confines of the wheelchair he was manoeuvring into the room —

Eyes which widened when they looked at Sabine, then became opaque — blank. The chair stopped, and the hands directing it tightened on the controls until the knuckles turned white. Suddenly, the room was filled with silence, threatening and highly charged.

It was like that endless moment, Sabine thought, between the lightning flash and the first crackle of thunder.

He said softly, 'Who are you?' and Sabine felt all the hairs stir on the back of her neck.

She lifted her chin, and stared back at him. 'My name is Sabine Russell, *monsieur.*'

'And you are Isabelle's daughter, of course.' A pause. 'How is your mother?'

Sabine said evenly, 'She died eight years ago, *monsieur,* when I was fourteen. I learned only recently that she'd lived near here.'

'And so you decided to pay us a visit.' She saw his hands relax, and the broad shoulders lean back in the chair. 'Well, that is natural. But someone should have told me that you were here,' he added, shooting a glance at Rohan, who stood, his face expressionless. 'I live very much in seclusion these days, *mademoiselle,* with my books and my papers. Yet when I returned to the house just now I sensed that something—unusual had occurred.'

He gave a wry smile. 'Of course, I understand now the reason for my poor wife's accident. Your resemblance to your mother is—quite amazing. I confess that when I came into the room more than twenty years—slipped away.'

Sabine bit her lip. 'I seem to have been a shock to a number of people. I didn't intend it.'

'Oh, not a shock, *mademoiselle.* More—a delightful surprise, wouldn't you say so, Rohan?'

Rohan shrugged, his eyes fixed watchfully on his uncle's face.

'But I should have been told of your arrival,' the *Baron* went on. 'So that I could welcome Isabelle's daughter to my house in person.'

Rohan drank the remainder of the wine in his glass and replaced it on the tray. He said, 'I thought you were still in Domme, Uncle. And Miss Russell was only able to pay a brief visit. She is just leaving.'

'But not before she has told me what she thinks of our wine,' the *Baron* said, smiling. 'I was told once that a good vintage should be like a woman — full-bodied and generous. Is ours ready to be — taken and enjoyed, do you think, *mademoiselle*?'

Sabine laughed. 'The '86 certainly,' she said. 'Although I can't approve of the sexist metaphor. The '89 needs to put on a little weight.'

'You hear?' The *Baron* looked at his nephew. 'Maybe Hercule has returned to us too.'

'No one has returned to us,' Rohan said curtly. 'Miss Russell is here on a short holiday, that's all. She will be going back to England very soon.'

'Then we must make the most of her. Perhaps you will dine with us, *mademoiselle,* on Saturday evening?'

'We cannot monopolise Miss Russell's time.' Rohan's frown was swift and disapproving. 'No doubt her plans are already made.'

'You must forgive Rohan's apparent churlishness,' Gaston de Rochefort said gently. 'Your mother's inexplicable desertion of my poor brother all those years ago still rankles with him.' He lifted a shoulder. 'But the heart has its reasons, and in any case Isabelle is beyond blame now.'

'That's exactly how I feel about it,' Sabine said, giving Rohan a defiant glance. 'Although I admit I'd like to know exactly what those reasons were.'

'Who can tell?' The *Baron* sighed. 'A lovers' quarrel—the natural nerves of a bride. One can find all kinds of explanations.'

'I suppose so,' Sabine said slowly. 'But with my mother it was more than that. I'm sure of it. It was if she wanted to forget that this part of her life ever existed.'

'You don't think maybe her wishes should be respected?' Rohan asked, a note of anger simmering just below the surface of his voice.

'She's been accused of a lot of things,' Sabine said coolly. 'I feel it's up to me to put the record straight.' She turned to the *Baron*. 'Thank you for your invitation, *monsieur*. I'd be happy to accept.'

'Then shall we say eight o'clock? But I hope you will visit us less formally before then. Where are you staying?'

'Miss Russell is using Les Hiboux,' Rohan said abruptly.

'But of course. A charming place, but a little primitive,' said the *Baron*. 'We have a swimming-pool at the rear of the house, Miss Russell, which you are welcome to use whenever you wish.' He turned to his nephew. 'Rohan, you must show Miss Russell the short-cut through the woods between our house and hers.'

Rohan's mouth tightened. 'It would be better if I asked Marie-Christine to point the way, Uncle Gaston, if that's what you wish.' He paused. 'We need to talk, you and I.'

Gaston de Rochefort was still smiling, but Sabine saw that tell-tale tightening of his hands on the controls of the chair. The tension in the room had changed in some way. 'You have been to Arrancay today, I suppose. The jewel of the Haut-Médoc.' He made it sound almost insulting.

'Yes,' Rohan said, wearily. 'But that's not important. At least not yet. It's the quotation from Lemaître I put on your desk two weeks ago that we have to discuss.'

'I've seen it,' the *Baron* said shortly. 'His prices are absurd. Our present casks can be scraped.'

'They have been,' Rohan said grittily. 'Too many times already. And we should also discuss the re-planting programme with Jacques.'

The *Baron* moved a hand dismissively. 'There is plenty of time for this later. You are always so impatient, my dear boy. And, besides, we should not bore Miss Russell with the business of the *vignoble*. Particularly when she wishes you to escort her back to Les Hiboux. It's not very gallant to keep her waiting,' he added reprovingly.

'Oh, please.' Sabine's face flamed. 'I can find my own way. . .'

'It doesn't matter,' Rohan said harshly. 'The *vignoble* has never been my uncle's top priority.'

For one inimical moment, the eyes of the two men met. Oh, Lord, Sabine thought, dismayed, the swords are out.

'*Touché.*' It was as if the *Baron* had picked up her thought. He was smiling ruefully, disarmingly. 'Rohan will tell you, *mademoiselle,* that I spend too much time on my researches. But when one has become — inactive some consolation is needed in life. And, I admit, the history of our region has become mine.'

'May I know what you're researching?' Sabine asked.

He gave a self-deprecating shrug. 'The role of the

local *bastides* in the Wars of Religion. I am writing a book on the subject.'

'I don't think I know what a *bastide* is.'

'They were fortified towns built in the Middle Ages, some by the French and some by the English, from which they preyed on each other, particularly during the Hundred Years' War between our countries. It was a violent and savage period, you understand. Later, in the sixteenth century, some of the *bastides* allied themselves with the Huguenot cause against the Catholics, and there was more bloodshed.'

'Not always,' Rohan put in drily, and the *Baron* laughed.

'Rohan is referring to a story he's always enjoyed about the men of Monpazier versus Villefranche de Périgord. They set off to raid each other on the same night, but passed somehow in the darkness. Of course, when each army arrived at the other's *bastide,* it found no defences, and looted as much as it wished. When light dawned, both sides looked very foolish, and made a treaty that everything should be put back exactly as it had been.'

Sabine laughed too. 'It's a nice story. I wish all wars could be settled as easily.' She paused. 'Are any of these *bastides* in the neighbourhood?'

'Monpazier — one of the most beautiful — is only a few kilometres away. Rohan has to go there tomorrow — some tiresome business with insurance. He would be glad to take you with him. There is an excellent restaurant where you could have lunch.'

'Oh, please.' Sabine shot an appalled glance at

Rohan's stony face. 'I don't want to be a nuisance. I can do my own sightseeing, really. . .'

'Oh, but I insist,' said Gaston de Rochefort. His smile was curiously sweet. 'There is no problem, is there, Rohan?'

'None at all,' Rohan said colourlessly, thrusting his hands into his pockets and turning away.

'That is settled, then.' The *Baron* sounded satisfied. '*A bientôt, mademoiselle.* Until Saturday.'

This is crazy, Sabine thought, as they went out into the sunshine. One moment, I'm being thrown off the premises. The next, I'm practically being adopted. Yet when he first saw me it was definitely scary. . . I don't understand any of it.

She stole a look at her companion. His eyes were brooding and his mouth compressed. She said, 'I'm sorry if I got in the way just now, when you wanted to talk about the vineyard.'

He shrugged. 'If you'd not been there, he would have found another excuse, believe me.'

'Oh.' Sabine digested that, then took a breath. 'Nor was I hinting for a guided tour. You—don't have to take me to Monpazier.'

'Those are the *Baron's* orders,' he said with cool indifference. 'It's best to comply. It makes life much easier,' he added with faint grimness. 'Besides, you'll probably have to face a full interrogation on the Monpazier *bastide* on Saturday. I'll pick you up at ten tomorrow morning.'

She looked down at the broad flags of the terrace they were crossing. 'But won't Antoinette object?'

He gave her a brief, incredulous look. 'Why should

she? She hasn't the slightest interest in Monpazier. She belongs, heart and soul, to Paris.'

'Oh,' was all she could think of to say. It would be a strange marriage, she thought, with Antoinette hitting the high spots in the big city, while her husband tended his vines here in the Périgord. But if that was what they both wanted. . .

It wouldn't suit me, she thought. I'd want to be with him, working alongside him. Sleeping with him at night.

From the terrace, a broad flight of central steps led down to lawns and formal flowerbeds. Ahead of them the dark shadow of the trees waited. She wasn't at all sure she wanted to be shown this short-cut through the woods, although Isabelle must have used it many times, when she was living at Les Hiboux and working at the château. She glanced back at the house. There seemed to be windows everywhere, like bright eyes, staring down at her, watching her every move.

She suppressed a shiver. 'It's very beautiful here,' she commented over-brightly in compensation.

'Yes, I suppose it must seem so.' Rohan roused himself from his abstraction and glanced round him. 'But I may have become blind to its charms. This place hasn't the happiest of associations for me.' He looked at her. 'Tell me something. Are you still glad you came here?'

'I'm neither glad nor sorry. It was something I felt I had to do.' She looked straight ahead, desperately aware of him beside her, conscious of the start of an unfamiliar and unwelcome ache of yearning deep within her. 'Although it hasn't been one of the happiest experiences of my life either,' she added in a low voice.

'What did you expect? One stone is disturbed on a hillside, and soon it becomes a landslide.' He shrugged again, almost angrily. 'Well, it is done, and there's no turning back now.'

She gave an uneven laugh. 'You make me sound like some kind of natural disaster.'

'Perhaps that's how I see you.' His mouth twisted. 'Like one of the summer hailstorms which come without warning and strip the fruit from the vines. One moment the sky is clear — then, on the horizon, one small insignificant cloud. And afterwards — one is left with the wreckage.'

They'd reached the trees now. There was a clearly defined path, but she still had to pick her way with care. Except for the rasp of the crickets, it was very quiet.

She said huskily, 'I didn't come here to wreck anything. Or to make any kind of demand. Whatever you may think or believe about my mother, you must understand that.'

'Perhaps Isabelle didn't intend it either. But it happened. Maybe she was the kind who trails havoc behind her wherever she goes.'

'And I'm her daughter, so naturally I must be the same,' Sabine said harshly. 'Well, she broke no hearts in England, and nor have I — ever. I didn't mean to make trouble here either.' She stared up into the sun-dappled leaves. 'In fact, if I'd known the effect my arrival was going to have, perhaps I'd have stayed away. I — I just don't know.'

Rohan halted, seizing her arm, and jerking her roughly round to face him. 'Then why did you come?' he grated. 'You don't want money. It can't have been mere curiosity. You're too determined — too single-minded about it for that. What is this — great truth you're looking for?'

She swallowed. 'I — I came to find my real father.'

There was a long silence, then he said wearily, '*Mon Dieu!*' and his hand fell from her arm. 'Are you saying that Isabelle was pregnant — that she was expecting Fabien's child when she ran away?'

She nodded.

'But it makes no sense.' He punched one hand against the other. 'Fabien loved her, and they were going to be married within weeks anyway. Plenty of babies come too soon after the wedding. People would just have shrugged their shoulders. There would have been no shame attached to either of them. Why should she have left him?'

'That's what I keep asking myself — because she didn't just leave. She hid in England, and never came back.'

'What are you implying? That she was afraid of something — afraid of my stepfather, perhaps?' He shook his head. 'That's impossible. He married my mother when I was just two years old. I never heard him raise his voice to her, and he mourned sincerely when she died. Children know these things — they have an instinct — they sense undercurrents.'

'Do they?' Sabine asked bitterly. 'I was totally oblivious. I never suspected a thing, even though my supposed father always kept me at arm's length.' She folded her arms across her body. 'Every time I called him Daddy, it must have been like twisting a knife in a wound,' she said, with a shiver. 'I tried so hard, you see, to give him extra attention — extra love — to try and make up for the loss of Maman. But it was never any use. I suppose I thought — if I found my real father he'd be — different somehow. He'd want me. . .'

Her voice cracked suddenly. With a soft groan, Rohan pulled her into his arms, holding her close against his body, the strong fingers stroking her hair with surprising gentleness.

'Quiet now,' he murmured. 'It's all right. Everything will be all right.'

Sabine's face was pressed against his chest. Gradually she found herself breathing the clean, laundered smell of his linen shirt, and the warmer, subtler scent of his skin, with a growing and bewildered delight. Her senses acknowledged the strength of the arms which held her, the power of his thigh muscles against her softer, more yielding flesh. The rhythm of his heartbeart seemed to echo her own, in some strange and miraculous conjunction, creating one shared, tumultuous pulse which filled the universe.

Her head said, *This is danger.* Her heart replied, *This is what I was born for.*

She felt her whole inner being convulse in a helpless, shattering pang of sheer physical longing, and she lifted dazed and dazzled eyes to look up at him. The caressing hand stilled, as he stared down into her face, reading the message of its new and raw vulnerability, and he made a harsh sound in his throat.

'In the name of God, Sabine, what are you trying to

do to me?' he muttered, then bent his head and kissed her quivering mouth with a deliberate and sensuous completeness.

One arm went round his neck, her fingers tangling in the silky hair at his nape. Her other hand was splayed against his shoulder, under his shirt, her fingertips discovering the glory of bone and muscle under the heated skin. She was coming alive in his arms, the frozen centre of pain and rejection deep within her melting under the urgency of his kiss. Somewhere close at hand a bird sang in a paean of thrilling and triumphant sweetness, and she heard its song echoed in her own heart.

His lips parted hers, and his tongue invaded her mouth, bathing it with liquid fire. At the same time, his hand slid the length of her spine with tingling and devastating slowness, to fasten on the curve of her hip, urging her body to an even more intimate pressure against his.

They might almost have been naked. She found herself wishing they were so in reality. Their light summer clothing was suddenly an intolerable barrier. As if he read her thought, Rohan's hand went to the front of her dress, tugging at the buttons which fastened it. Uncaring, she felt one and then another tear from the fabric under his impatient fingers. Her eyes closed, and her head fell back, as she waited in a kind of sensual anguish. . .

From some different world, she heard the bird's song cease abruptly in mid-trill, and the startled flutter of its wings as it took flight, followed by the soft rustle of a breeze through the bushes.

Except there was no breeze. The afternoon was still. Even the crickets had fallen silent.

And in that silence a whisper, hardly more than a breath: 'Isabelle's daughter.'

CHAPTER SIX

SABINE pulled away from him, her head turning sharply, as she tried to drag her reeling senses together.

'What is it?' Rohan reached for her again, but she took a step backwards, staring round her, straining her ears.

'I heard something—someone—I don't know.'

He listened too, then shook his head. 'There's nothing.'

'Not now,' she said hoarsely. 'But the crickets stopped and the bird flew away, quite suddenly. There was—there must have been—someone in those bushes over there.'

Rohan's brows lifted. 'There's no need to play games.' His voice was cool. 'If you've had second thoughts about letting me touch you, then just say so.'

'It isn't that.' She felt wretched, her body and emotions in turmoil. 'I did hear something. At least, I thought I did.'

Rohan gave her a long look, then strode over to the clump of bushes she indicated. 'There's no sign of anything now.' He came back unsmilingly to her side. 'Your imagination must have been playing tricks.' His mouth twisted sardonically. 'Or was it just your way of halting a situation that was getting out of control?'

Her face warmed. 'No. And please don't flatter yourself.'

'I don't,' he said. 'I wanted you, and I think you
wanted me, until you realised we were getting near the
point of no return, and you chickened out.' He shook
his head. 'What the hell did you think — that I was
going to take you here on the ground — or up against
some tree? Give me credit for a little more finesse than
that.'

Finesse, Sabine thought bewilderedly. What did
finesse have to do with that wild upsurge of feeling
which had almost overwhelmed her? It was too calcu-
lated a word to describe what had happened between
them. It implied a deliberate technique — a sexual
expertise designed to beguile and seduce. . .

She stopped right there, as the truth dawned on her.
Because Rohan hadn't been overwhelmed at all — had
he? He'd known exactly what he was doing all along.

'*I think you wanted me*'. Hardly the reaction of a
man caught in the grip of a blinding and irresistible
desire.

Yet it was, she thought, horrified. I was crazy for
him. He made me forget everything — even that he
belongs to someone else — that he's going to be married
in just a few weeks. If I hadn't heard that whisper, I'd
have let him do what he wanted — anything he
wanted — right here and now.

Her stomach lurched as she realised how near she'd
come to disaster. However much she'd fallen in love
with Rohan, to him she was no more than a passing
fancy, to be enjoyed then discarded. Like her mother
before her, she could have ended up back in England,
alone and pregnant.

Well, she would fall out of love with him. It couldn't

be love, anyway, it had all happened too fast. It was just infatuation, and could be controlled. I will not live at the mercy of my hormones, she told herself savagely. It occurred to her that it could have been Antoinette herself watching them, but she dismissed that almost at once. Even after one brief meeting she knew that Rohan's future wife wasn't the type to creep tamely away to avoid discovery. She would have erupted from concealment, all guns blazing, and made the ultimate scene.

Perhaps there hadn't been anyone there, after all. Maybe what she'd really heard was the voice of her own conscience.

'How pale you've become,' Rohan said more gently, and his hand touched her cheek. 'You've had a shock, haven't you? You really believe someone was spying on us.'

'The real thing that shocks me is my own stupidity,' Sabine said curtly, brushing away the caressing hand. 'I can't believe I actually stood here and let you — maul me.'

He was very still suddenly. 'Is that how it was? It didn't seem to me you were quite so passive.'

'You're the expert, of course,' she threw back at him. 'The one with finesse. I'm sure you don't get many refusals.'

'Perhaps I don't ask that often, either.' He answered her anger with his own.

'Am I supposed to feel flattered now?'

'Feel what the hell you like. But next time you're with a man warn him in advance that you like to change your mind, and play the tease, or there could be trouble.'

'I do not,' she said tautly, 'make a habit of behaving like this. You—you took advantage of me at a moment of weakness.'

His brows lifted. 'Truly? Well, if you plan any more such moments, have them when I'm not around.' He paused. 'I'm glad to see you've regained your colour.'

'Along with my sense of decency,' Sabine returned brusquely. 'And now I'm going back to the house— alone.'

He laughed. 'Running away?' he mocked. 'Isabelle's daughter.'

The gibe assailed her like a blow to the pit of the stomach. She knew with total certainty that her imagination hadn't been playing tricks, and that it was the second time in only a few minutes that she'd heard those precise words.

She said in a suffocated voice, 'Don't—don't say that.'

His eyes narrowed. 'What is it? What's the matter?' He took a step towards her, and Sabine recoiled.

'Just leave me alone.'

'As you wish,' he said icily. He pointed through the trees. 'If you follow this path, you'll come out by the farm.' He turned away, then halted, looking back at her over his shoulder. 'And if you intend to come this way regularly wear more sensible shoes,' he added curtly. 'We have snakes in the Périgord.'

'Including human ones,' she bawled childishly at his retreating back, fighting down an instinctive gasp of revulsion.

She watched him disappear from view, then stood for a moment, forcing herself to breathe deeply and evenly. Instinct was telling her to collapse against the nearest tree and cry like a baby, but instinct could go and chase itself. It had betrayed her badly once today already.

When her legs had stopped shaking sufficiently, she started off down the path again. Every bush seemed to be having its own deliberate rustle as she passed, she realised wryly, wondering whether unseen whispers were marginally better or worse than snakes, or other wildlife.

She felt bitterly ashamed of the way she'd fallen into Rohan's arms. Feeling as she did, and knowing he was committed elsewhere, she should have kept her distance. All she could summon in her defence was that she'd hurt no one but herself. And that was no excuse, and little comfort, she thought.

And tomorrow she was supposed to be visiting the Monpazier *bastide* with him. She couldn't imagine the trip would still take place. No doubt the morning would bring a polite message of regret, and that would be that. Although she still had Saturday evening's dinner to face, she reminded herself. Unless she cut her losses and went back to England. That was an option gaining in appeal with every breath she took. After all, she now knew beyond reasonable doubt who her father had been, and she'd warmed to the little she'd been told about him. Surely it would be better to content herself with that than stay on, laying herself open to inevitable heartbreak.

When eventually the path forked abruptly, she

paused to get her bearings. She guessed her own route
lay straight ahead and downhill, but a glance to her left
offered a glimpse of stonework through the trees. That,
she supposed, must be the legendary tower. It might
be out of bounds, but the temptation to take a slightly
closer look was a temptation she could not resist.

The ferns and undergrowth met almost waist-high
across the path, and she had to push her way through
them to reach her goal. The tower itself stood, three-
storeyed and square, in the middle of a clearing. The
roof had collapsed long ago, leaving some of its timbers
exposed to the elements, but apart from that it seemed
reasonably stable. Access was gained by an iron-
studded wooden door, which was shut, but not pad-
locked or chained up, as far as Sabine could see.
Perhaps the *Baron's* word was considered sufficient
deterrent to would-be explorers.

She walked across the clearing. No bars on the
windows now, but a rose in full bloom had been
allowed to grow unchecked up one of the walls—
perhaps a descendant of the rose the erring de
Rochefort wife of centuries ago had used to signal to
her lover.

Sabine still found it astonishing that the family
weren't making more use of the legend to promote
their wine. She could see how easily it could be done.
Tidy up the clearing, she thought, repair the masonry,
if it needs it, and conduct the wine-tastings here, in the
open air if possible, or in the tower itself. Even have
some mock-medieval manuscripts printed telling the
story—at least the version with the happy ending—and
give every woman in the party a rose on departure.

Oh, there were all kinds if things that could be done to make the visit memorable. Surely Gaston de Rochefort with his love of history could see that?

She grasped the heavy iron handle and turned it cautiously. If a slab of stone fell on her head now and flattened her, it would serve her right for prying, she thought wryly, as the door opened slowly and reluctantly with a grudging squeal of rusty hinges.

The room was festooned with cobwebs, the air musty and thick with dust and disuse. What light there was filtered uneasily through slit-like windows, high in the wall, and there were traces of animal droppings on the floor. Probably rats, she thought, grimacing. The atmosphere of neglect and abandonment was almost tangible.

But it had clearly been used at some time in the past. A huge, elderly sofa, its upholstery stained, torn, and oozing stuffing, stood in the centre of the room. A small table lay on its side, with one broken leg, and a narrow dresser, its cupboard doors hanging open, stood against one wall.

Perhaps they used to picnic here, Sabine thought. I wonder why they stopped? She paused, shivering suddenly. Because she knew why. Could understand completely why no one came here any more. There was a sadness in the room, a feeling of oppression, that had nothing to do with the years of dirt and disarray. It permeated the stones and filled every corner with shadows. She could well believe that the betrayed husband had taken his ultimate revenge centuries before. There'd been no happy endings here.

She looked at the narrow flight of stone stairs leading

to the upper floors, and knew that wild horses wouldn't drag her up them. She backed out of the door, and closed it securely again. The tower was a disturbing place, but so was the whole of La Tour Monchauzet, for that matter. There were too many shadows obscuring its past, and still blurring the present. She could understand why Isabelle had wanted none of it and chosen Les Hiboux instead.

As she started back across the clearing, she found she was walking faster and faster all the time. The compulsion to get away, and not look back, was as strong as a hand on her shoulder urging her forward. And when she reached the path down to the farm she began to run.

She was breathless by the time she reached the farm. At the sound of her flying footsteps, a small dog trotted out and barked at her, and a woman emerged from the farmhouse itself, shading her eyes against the sun. She was dark, *petite* and *soignée*, and her smile, though warm, held a hint of reproof, as Sabine came to a halt, gasping, her hand pressed to her side.

'Miss Russell. I knew it must be. But it's not wise to exercise so violently in such heat.' She held out her hand. 'I am Monique Lavaux. I have been left an agitated message from my niece Marie-Christine telling me that you are camping at Les Hiboux, without chairs or even the bare necessities of life.'

'That's a bit of an exaggeration.' Sabine returned her smile. 'It was my own choice to stay there, when I could have gone to a hotel.' She pulled a face. 'It— hasn't made me very popular in some quarters.'

'No, I can imagine that.' Monique Lavaux bent,

scooping the small dog up into her arms. She looked at
Sabine with frank wistfulness. 'Your mother and I were
friends from our schooldays. For a moment—as you
ran down the hill. . .' She paused. 'Seeing you here—
alone—is a sadness for me. I thought—we always
believed, Fabien and I—that Isabelle would come back
one day.'

She sighed, then said more briskly, 'But come in,
and have a drink with me—I've just made some fresh
lemonade—and we'll talk about the furniture. It's
stored in a depot in Monpazier at the moment. But
I've packed up a bundle of bedding—towels—things
like that for you to use in the meantime.'

'That's very kind of you.' Sabine followed her to the
shade of the veranda, and took the cushioned chair her
hostess indicated. Monique Lavaux deposited the dog
at her feet and vanished into the house, to return
almost immediately with a tall jug, clanking with ice,
and two tumblers.

'Your niece said you've been to Paris,' Sabine said
as the lemonade was poured.

'Yes.' She pulled a face. 'But I regard it as a penance.
I do not like cities, even one as beautiful as Paris. I am
only ever happy at home here in the Périgord.'

'I can understand that,' Sabine said, looking around
her.

'You feel it too.' Monique Lavaux nodded her
satisfaction. 'It's no wonder. This region after all is the
cradle of civilisation. Prehistoric man chose to live here
because he knew it was unique, endowed with everything he could ever need to survive and thrive.' She

smiled at Sabine. 'You have heard, of course, of our famous caves at Lascaux.'

'I've heard of them,' Sabine said. 'But haven't they been closed to visitors?'

'Alas, yes, because the wall paintings were beginning to deteriorate. Only archaeologists and scholars are allowed to visit now, in small, strictly limited groups. But for the rest of us they've built an exact replica near by at Lascaux Two.' She shrugged. 'But if you prefer to visit a real cave the complex at Les Eyzies is fascinating, and less restricted.'

'I haven't done any sightseeing yet,' Sabine confessed. 'But I really must before I go——' She'd been about to say 'home' but substituted 'back' instead.

'You're returning to England soon?' Mademoiselle Lavaux stared at her. 'But you've only just arrived. And what do you intend to do with the house?'

'I haven't even given that a thought. Finding it existed was enough of a shock.' She briefly outlined the events which had brought her to France, omitting, however, for the time being, the question mark over her parentage.

'I wanted to find out why Maman had kept the past such a big secret, but all I seem to have done is spook everyone—even you,' she said wryly. She paused. 'Do—do you condemn her too, *mademoiselle*, for running away as she did?'

'No,' Monique Lavaux said slowly. 'But I wish she had confided in me—told me her reasons. Perhaps I could have dissuaded her. I was so happy that she and Fabien had found each other again, even though there were still obstacles. And Isabelle seemed content too, at last.' She sighed. 'But when Fabien went to California things changed. She became nervous, *distraite*, almost as if she was frightened of something.'

She shrugged. 'I can only think she decided she could not marry Fabien after all, but could not bear to tell him so either. And yet he was so kind — so understanding. He would not have blamed her. But to return and find her gone, without a word, without a trace, was devastating for him.'

'Didn't he try to find her?'

'He was too ill. After the quarrel with his family, he had a nervous collapse. He spent months recovering in a private clinic in Bordeaux. When he came back, he was different. It was as if the old Fabien had died, and another man was living in his skin, pretending to be him, but without his spirit — his soul.'

'Why did he quarrel with his family? You'd have thought they'd have rallied round him — given him their support.'

'*Au contraire*.' Monique Lavaux's tone was dry. 'I believe they behaved as if he'd had a fortunate escape — condemned Isabelle as an *aventurière*, and worse. Terrible words were exchanged. Unforgivable things were said.

'That, of course, is why, when he returned from the clinic, he came to live alone at Les Hiboux. If Isabelle returned, he said, she should not find her home empty and unloved.' She bit her lip, the dark eyes suddenly very bright.

'And the château had become anathema to him,' she went on after a moment. 'He continued to visit his mother until her death, but I don't think he and Gaston ever spoke to each other again.'

Sabine's lips parted in a soundless gasp. 'But I talked to the *Baron* earlier, and Madame de Rochefort. They didn't say anything about a rift. . .'

'Naturally, they would not. It is hardly to their credit, after all. I thought, perhaps, when Gaston had his terrible accident, that there might be some softening — some attempt at a reconciliation, but I was wrong. Fabien was like stone.

'Because of his illness, he had lost Rohan, who went back to live with his grandfather at Arrancay. That was another severe blow. He and the boy adored each other. The vines eventually became his salvation. He'd taken over from Hercule Riquard as *maître de chai*, and he poured his whole life into promoting La Tour Monchauzet wines into a class of their own. He had a sense of the land — the weather. He left the grapes on the vine as long as possible — sometimes even late into October — but he never lost a vintage through frost.'

'Well, I'm glad something went right.' Sabine shook her head. 'What a catalogue of doom and disaster it's been, otherwise.

Monique Lavaux smiled a little. 'I suppose it must seem so.' She hesitated. 'But truly, after Isabelle's departure, it often seemed as if the family had been cursed.' She gave a little shiver, then laughed. 'But that is fanciful.'

Sabine remembered the tower and its shadows, and thought, I wonder. . . Trying to keep her voice casual, she said, 'When did Rohan—Monsieur Saint Yves come back from Arrancay?'

'When his stepfather's health began to suffer. Fabien wanted the *vignoble* to be run by someone in sympathy with his aims, who would continue with the modernisation process he'd started, and produce wine of the same quality. Rohan was the obvious choice, although his grandfather was reluctant to let him go, I think.' Mademoiselle Lavaux shook her head. 'But he has no easy task.'

She insisted on helping Sabine carry the bundles of bedding over to Les Hiboux. Standing in the *salon*, she looked around her wistfully. 'It is sad to see all this emptiness, and remember how it used to be.' She paused. 'It is a house that needs to be lived in. What will you do with it, do you think? Will you take up residence in France?'

'I don't think I can afford to—not immediately anyway. I work as a freelance translator, and I'd have to find out what opportunities there are here before I could decide.'

'Well, then, would you consider renting the house to a holiday company, perhaps? There is always demand among tourists for property such as this.'

'It hadn't occurred to me,' Sabine admitted. 'But it could be a solution.' She looked round her. 'I have to admit I don't want to sell up, not at once, anyway, when I've just found the place.'

'Of course not.' Monique Lavaux smiled understandingly, then became brisk again. 'However, if you wish to sell, I work as an estate agent, and I could help. But I think you should look over the stored furniture before you come to any decision. Some of the pieces are from Hercule's family, and are very old.' She produced a business card from her bag, and wrote an address on the back of it. 'Speak to Monsieur Pallon, and he will show you what there is.'

Sabine took the card. 'Has the furniture been in store for very long?' she asked doubtfully. 'Is there an account I should pay?'

'No, no. It has all been paid from Fabien's estate, also the local taxes and the charge for water and electricity. Everything had to be maintained just as it had been — for the day when Isabelle returned to Les Hiboux. Those were his orders.'

'That's a wonderful thing to have done.' Sabine's eyes shone.

Monique Lavaux smiled. 'Ah,' she said. 'But he was a wonderful person.'

She was in love with him, Sabine realised, with the insight of her own pain. And he probably never knew it. She said, with a catch in her voice, 'I — I wish very much that I'd been able to meet him.'

Mademoiselle Lavaux patted Sabine's shoulder, then glanced at her watch. 'Is there anything more I can do to help? No? Then I must be going. If you have no plans for tomorrow evening, perhaps you would like to have dinner with us.' She gave a pleased smile at Sabine's delighted acceptance, and disappeared purposefully back to the farm.

Sabine put her chicken casserole on to cook, then made up her bed. It would be good to sleep in real sheets tonight, she thought.

But when she eventually went to bed after a leisurely

supper sleep proved elusive. Her body was weary but her brain was buzzing, trying to make sense of everything she'd seen and heard that day. And at the forefront of her mind was Rohan Saint Yves.

The sadness in Monique Lavaux's eyes had emphasised to her that there was no future in allowing herself to love a man who was committed to another woman.

I shouldn't have allowed him anywhere near me, she told herself bitterly. I've been a fool and more than a fool. Becuase even if Antoinette didn't exist Rohan wouldn't involve himself with me—at least not seriously. To him, I'm just my mother's daughter, unworthy of trust or respect.

Although that didn't necessarily mean he wouldn't take anything she was unwise enough to offer, she reminded herself. So the most sensible thing to do was ignore her treacherous emotions and avoid Rohan's company altogether from now on. For one thing, she wouldn't wait for him to cancel their trip to Monpazier. She'd do it first. In the morning, she'd ask Marie-Christine to take him a note, saying that she'd had to make other plans. She'd leave early and go to Les Eyzies as Mademoiselle Lavaux had suggested, or perhaps to La Roque-Gageac, said to be the most beautiful village in France. She probably couldn't avoid having dinner at the château, but at least she wouldn't be alone with him there.

The actual composition of the note, over coffee the next morning, took a lot of thought, and several sheets of paper. She didn't want to sound rude, she thought, just—firm, letting him know without ambiguity that she wasn't available.

She put on a straight yellow skirt, just brushing her knee, and a matching vest-top. Even replica caves might be cold, she thought, slinging a yellow and white striped cotton blazer over her arm, and picking up her bag and camera on the way out to the car.

A swift call at the farm, and then freedom, she told herself, as she walked under the arch.

Bonjour.' He was leaning casually against her car, very much at his ease in the morning sunshine. 'Isn't it a beautiful day?'

'No,' Sabine said hoarsely. 'I mean—what are you doing here?'

'Something told me you might wish to make an earlier start than we'd planned.' The hooded eyes surveyed her with frank appreciation mingled with amusement. 'I see I was right.'

Sabine bit her lip. 'Actually, I've decided to leave Monpazier to another day. You—you have business to attend to—and I should only be in the way.'

'Then my business can wait too,' he said. 'Where do you wish to go instead?'

There was silence, then she said unevenly, 'You're not making this very easy for me.'

He shrugged. 'We have a date. You're trying to stand me up. Why should I make it easy?' He straightened. He said quietly, 'Sabine, I am trying, clumsily perhaps, to make amends for everything that has happened. I would like you to spend the day with me, please. Just a few hours looking round the *bastide* and having a meal together. Nothing more, I promise.' His smile was as warm as the sun. It beckoned—cajoled. 'Please,' he repeated.

A sweet, dizzying weakness swamped her body. Under the concealing folds of the blazer, her tightly clenched hands were trembling. It was madness. It was danger, and she knew it. She should walk away.

'I wrote you a note.' She held out the letter.

'I guessed you would.' He took it from her, tore it across, and threw the pieces away. His eyes challenged her. 'Now, tell me to my face that you don't want to come with me.'

The clamour of her heartbeat filled the silence between them, as she struggled to find the words that would send him away forever. But they wouldn't come.

She said on a little sigh, 'I — can't say that.'

'Then let's waste no more time.' He walked over to his car, parked near by and opened the passenger door for her. 'We're spending the day together,' he said softly, urgently, as Sabine got into the car, taking care not to brush against him. 'That's all.'

And that was the problem, Sabine thought, staring rigidly ahead of her as he started the car. It was — only a day to him, but to her. . . She shivered. To her, it was the beginning of the rest of her life — alone.

CHAPTER SEVEN

THEY took the road from Villereal, approaching Monpazier from the south. It was a fast journey, and accomplished for the most part in silence, although Rohan did point out the entrance to the Château de Biron, as they flashed past.

The château was in the process of being restored by the *département* of the Dordogne, he told her.

'It is quite an operation,' he added drily. 'Every generation of the Gontaut-Biron family added something to it since it began in the twelfth century. There are now fifteen different buildings, including the biggest vaulted kitchens in France.'

'I'll have to add it to my list,' she said. 'Although I doubt whether I'll have time to fit everything in.'

'How long are you planning to stay?' The question was clearly casual, his attention fixed firmly on the road ahead.

'I—haven't decided yet,' she said after a brief hesitation.

'You have work, of course?' He too paused. 'A— life to return to in England?'

'Very much so,' she returned composedly. He was probing, she realised, trying to discover if that 'life' included a man. Well, he could keep guessing.

'What is your work?'

'I'm a translator—not just for French, but Spanish

and Italian as well, and a little Portuguese. Although I'm basically a freelance, most of my work comes through various agencies.'

'It's a good living for you?'

She shrugged. 'I've no complaints.'

'You have no ambitions to work abroad — in Brussels for instance, or Strasbourg?'

'It's something I've considered. But I'd rather gain a little more experience first. Or I'd thought of getting a teaching qualification — maybe starting my own commercial language school.' She made herself sound enthusiastic, bursting with ideas. 'Now that Europe's really opened up, the sky's the limit.'

A steep hill wound sharply upwards into Monpazier. Rohan parked the car under some trees just outside the main wall, then they walked together through an arched gateway, and up the shaded street, passing between tall houses, their windows firmly shuttered against the intrusive sun, intermingled with shops.

A door in a wall stood slightly ajar, and Sabine glimpsed the enclosed grassy courtyard of someone's garden, like an emerald set in grey stone. There were flowers everywhere in tubs and window-boxes, and music played softly over speakers placed at strategic points.

Rohan was speaking. 'All the *bastides* were built like grids, with the streets crossing each other at right angles. The emphasis was on defence, you understand. It was essential that the walls could be manned fast in time of emergency.

'Monpazier, in fact, was built for the King of

England, Edward the First, and one of its hotels is even named for him.'

Sabine's brow was furrowed. 'But why was that? Surely the English and French were nearly always at war in those days.'

'The whole of Aquitaine belonged to the English crown, through the great Duchess Eleanor,' Rohan explained. 'She was the Queen of France and the most beautiful and fascinating woman in Europe, but she fell out of love with her husband on a crusade to the Holy Land, when she met Henry the Second of England, who was much younger than her.'

'And I thought toy boys were a modern invention.' Sabine's lips twitched in amusement. 'So what happened?'

'Didn't you learn history when you were at school?' Rohan's brows lifted in mock censure.

'Yes,' she admitted. 'But we seemed to concentrate on the economic effects of the Industrial Revolution, and stuff like that. The love-affairs of kings and queens would have been far more interesting.'

He laughed. 'I can believe it. Well, Eleanor divorced King Louis, who preferred religion to women anyway, and married Henry, who then became Duke of Aquitaine through her. Although he and his son Richard Coeur de Lion had to fight all their lives to maintain the title, and Edouard Premier too when his time came,' he added.

'Eleanor adored the Périgord. She established the Courts of Love in Aquitaine, where women were worshipped almost like goddesses.'

'And she was chief goddess, I suppose,' Sabine commented.

'Of course. A troubadour once sang of her that if he possessed the whole world he would sacrifice it to hold the Queen of England in his arms for just one night.'

'How wonderful to be able to inspire such devotion,' Sabine said slowly.

He shot her an amused glance. 'You don't think a man could feel so deeply for a woman these days?'

'It would be nice to think so.' She shrugged. 'But I doubt it.'

'But here in the land of the troubadours,' he said softly, 'anything is possible.'

Avoiding his suddenly intent look, Sabine transferred her attention across the road. 'I suppose that's the main church!' she exclaimed brightly. 'It's enormous.'

'And also very old.' The dry note in his voice told her he was perfectly aware of her manoeuvre. 'It was begun in the thirteenth century and there's a famous inscription above the door.'

Sabine stared up at the lettering cut into the ancient stonework. '"The people of France recognise the existence of the Supreme Being, and the immortality of the soul,"' she read slowly. 'What's so unusual about that?'

'It was put there during the Revolution,' Rohan returned. 'At a time when the Church and religious belief were under a great deal of pressure. But the people of the Dordogne have always had a reputation for being independent thinkers.'

He slid a casual hand under her elbow and guided her up the street towards another arched gateway.

'Now you'll see why Monpazier was known as England's pearl,' he said softly.

This was the heart of the *bastide*, Sabine realised with a gasp of delight. It was a big central square, completely surrounded by covered arcades above which rose the creamy stones of the original medieval houses, topped by the steeply sloping, earth-red roofs.

For a moment, the centuries seemed to roll away, and she could visualise grim-faced men in chain-mail racing to answer some alarm, while women in wimpled head-dresses leaned down from the Gothic windows to bid them Godspeed.

The present-day ambience was slightly more prosaic. The shadows of the arcades sheltered the façades of modern shops, and directly below their arches stone benches and troughs of flowering plants had been placed. Instead of soldiers, tourists armed only with cameras patrolled the freshly washed cobbles of the square, while, outside the various restaurants and the *tabac* on the corner, tables with bright umbrellas were being set out in the sunshine.

Directly opposite was a timbered market hall similar to the one in Villereal, where the original grain measures could still be seen, Rohan told her. There was a local market every Thursday, and, in addition, each spring and summer Monpazier was the centre for a giant mushroom fair. No one in the square seemed to be in a hurry, but a purposeful bustle of activity permeated the atmosphere just the same.

'Would you like some coffee?' Rohan guided Sabine to one of the tables outside the *tabac*. He gave the order, then leaned back in his chair, smiling at her. 'Well?'

'It's incredible,' she admitted. 'One of the loveliest places I've ever seen. And so peaceful.'

'It wasn't always like this,' he said. 'Monpazier has a chequered history, torn between French and English, Catholic and Protestant. The *place* here hasn't always been so welcoming, believe me. In the seventeenth century a weaver called Buffarot led a local revolt, and was broken on the wheel only a few metres from where we're sitting.'

Sabine shuddered. 'How terrible.'

'They were terrible times. But Monpazier seems now to be at peace with its past.' He paused. 'Perhaps it's a lesson we should all learn.'

'Maybe.' She looked down at the spotless white surface of the table. 'Does that mean you're prepared to forgive Maman for — leaving as she did?'

'I said I never would.' His face was grave. 'It wasn't just Fabien who was hurt, you understand. I was a child who'd lost his own mother, and was looking for affection. With Fabien and Isabelle I was promised a family again.' He shrugged. 'I wondered so often whether it was my fault that Isabelle went. Whether she could not face the thought of having a stepson foisted on her.'

'No,' Sabine said instantly. 'I know that's not true. I found a photograph of you among her things. She wouldn't have kept that, if she hadn't loved you.' She took the folder from her bag and passed it across to him. 'Do you remember this?'

His face softened. 'Yes, I remember. Antoinette was

being a pest, as usual, and Tante Héloise was scolding me for not wanting to play with her.'

Sabine closed her bag carefully. 'You and Antoinette were — brought up together, I understand.'

'For a while — until I was sent back to Arrancay.' He spoke almost absently, his attention concentrated on the photographs in front of him. She saw his face change, his brows snap together.

She saw what he was looking at — the man, standing alone. She said gently, 'She kept that too. I've just realised where it was taken. It's the tower, isn't it?'

There was a silence, then Rohan said, 'Yes — the tower.' His voice and face were bleak. 'Have you shown these to anyone else?'

'No. I thought they might — distress people, in the circumstances. And they've upset you, haven't they?'

'Yes.' He put out a hand and touched hers. 'But not for the reason you think. You've done nothing wrong, believe me.' He sighed quickly and sharply and put the photographs back in the folder. 'May I keep these for a while?'

'Yes, of course,' she said, as the coffee arrived. She hesitated. 'Is something the matter?'

'Yes,' he said. 'But I can't explain — at least not yet.' His eyes looked deeply into hers. 'Can you be patient and trust me?'

'I hardly know you.' The warm tingling confusion was back, turning her mind to jelly and her legs to water.

'That's true,' he said. 'Yet in some ways we seem to have known each other forever. That all our lives we've been waiting to meet. I think you feel that too.'

She picked up her coffee-cup hurriedly and drank some, burning her mouth. 'Rohan, don't, please.' She was falling over her words. 'It doesn't matter what I think. You—you mustn't talk like that. . .'

'Why not?'

'Because people——' she couldn't bring herself to say Antoinette's name '—are going to be hurt, and you know it.' She took a breath. 'You're not free.'

'Not at the moment. I won't pretend there aren't problems, but nothing we can't overcome together.'

'Ever since I came here, I've been called Isabelle's daughter virtually as a term of abuse.' Her voice shook slightly. 'I don't want to be accused of causing havoc in my turn.'

'I think that was inevitable from the moment you arrived in France,' he said quietly. 'But we can't discuss it now. I have my appointment to keep.' He pointed down a street leading off the corner of the square where they were sitting. 'Meet me at the restaurant at the bottom at twelve.' He got to his feet, leaving a handful of coins for the bill, then came round to her, bending to give her a swift, hard kiss on the mouth before striding off.

Sabine watched him go, prey to all kinds of conflicting emotions. Part of her mind, the cool, rational fragment, was insisting that it was all happening too fast and too soon. Yet blind instinct told her that Rohan was her man, and had been since time began. All they'd had to do, as he said, was recognise each other.

But he still belongs to Antoinette, she thought achingly. We can't hurt her—humiliate her like this when she's expecting to marry him in just a few weeks, even if it has been arranged for family reasons, and not for love. There's been too much bitterness already.

Certainly, there wasn't an atom of tenderness in his voice when he spoke of her, but what did that prove? They were used to each other, and Antoinette was undoubtedly physically desirable. A lot of marriages staggered along with less.

Yet if Rohan did marry Antoinette, caring nothing for her, that would make three wretched people instead of one. She sighed soundlessly. What a mess it all was. But Rohan had told her to trust him, and that's what she had to do.

She finished her coffee, and set off to explore the town. As well as the usual souvenirs, she found a shop selling interesting ceramics, and treated herself to a pair of pottery owls. There were also numerous local specialities on sale including *pâté de foie gras*, and tins of *confit* — goose and duck preserved in their own fat, and the famous walnut liqueur, while a small art gallery offered original oil-paintings and water-colours, including views of Monpazier itself.

She bought some postcards, and an illustrated book on the *bastides* of the Dordogne from the local newsagent, and spent a mouth-watering few moments coveting the strawberry, peach and raspberry tarts displayed in a *pâtisserie* window.

She was just coming out of Credit Agricole, having cashed some traveller's cheques, when she saw Antoinette emerging from the *pharmacie* opposite. She checked instantly, but it was too late. She'd been seen.

'So, it's you.' The other girl's face and tone were equally ungracious. 'What are you doing here?'

'Sightseeing,' Sabine returned shortly, wondering if she looked as guilty as she felt.

'I thought you were supposed to be leaving for England. Tante Héloise said there was nothing for you here, and that you'd soon be gone.'

'In my own good time,' Sabine said levelly.

Antoinette tossed her head. 'I should be ashamed to stay where I wasn't wanted. But that's what your mother did, of course. She was just a common slut, making trouble, just like you — chasing other women's men.' Her tone seethed with poison. 'I've heard all about her — everything. I know what you're trying to do, and it won't work. You're trying to take Rohan away from me.'

'I don't have to listen to this.' Sabine swallowed, desperately aware that their altercation was attracting the attention of other customers to the bank.

'I'm warning you.' Antoinette pushed her face, distorted with temper, towards Sabine's, forcing her to recoil. 'Go away from here, and leave Rohan alone, or it will be the worse for you. I've wanted him all my life, and I can give him in return what he most desires — La Tour Monchauzet. That's what counts with Rohan — the vines. Becoming one of the the great *vignerons* of the south-west. That's his real passion, you stupid bitch. I realised it long ago. And you're not going to interfere, and spoil things.' She turned on her heel, and stormed off, pausing only to hurl, 'Isabelle's daughter,' over her shoulder, in a voice which rang with contempt.

Sabine felt physically sick as she watched her go. The unseen watcher. The whisperer in the woods. Incredibly, that must have been Antoinette after all. She felt as if she'd been dipped in slime.

Somewhere a bell rang out in the age-old call of the Angelus, reminding her that it was midday and she had to meet Rohan. But how could she — feeling as she did?

If she had her own car, she knew she'd have turned tail and run, back to Les Hiboux to begin with, and then to Bordeaux and its airport. She felt totally unnerved by the encounter, and wasn't ashamed to admit it.

When she arrived at the restaurant, Rohan was waiting in the doorway with open impatience.

'I thought you were lost,' he laughed, kissing her hand and then her lips. He saw her pallor and the trouble in her eyes, and frowned. 'What is it, *chérie*? What's happened?'

'It's Antoinette. She knows about us. She made a horrible scene outside the bank.' Her voice was toneless.

'Antoinette has made a speciality of horrible scenes since her birth,' he said grimly. 'I hope you told her that our relationship was none of her affair?'

'How could I?' she challenged. 'She has a right to be angry. She's your fiancée, after all.'

He stared at her, his brows snapping together ferociously. 'What did you say?' The question exploded out of him.

She said wearily, 'Rohan — you told me yourself you were going to be married in a few weeks.'

He said forcefully, '*Dieu*! I need a drink. We both

do,' and almost dragged her into the restaurant's bar. He ordered a *pastis* for himself and a *pineau de Charentes* for Sabine, then sat down with her at a table in the corner.

'Now listen to me,' he said quietly. 'And listen well. I am not marrying Antoinette. I am not such a fool. Oh, the idea has been put to me many times. I admit it. We've known each other since childhood, after all, so it would be convenient, and make good sense. I know all the arguments.' He paused. 'But it would also be a living hell. You could not have thought that I had ever considered her as my wife. Did I ever give the slightest sign. . .?'

'No,' she admitted. 'But when we were in the great chamber you mentioned a wedding — in a few weeks.' Her voice was small. 'So I assumed. . .'

He groaned. 'Not mine, little fool. Marie-Christine is marrying Jacques. They've been engaged for a year, and it was decided the wedding could take place during August, when there is just routine spraying and pruning to be done, well before the *vendange* itself, when I cannot do without him.'

'Marie-Christine,' she repeated. 'And — Jacques. The Jacques who drove me to Les Hiboux?'

'Yes,' he said, and she nodded slowly.

'I'm glad.'

'So am I.' He reached across the table and raised her hand to his lips. 'We'll dance together at their wedding, you and I,' he said softly, and the promise in his voice brought a warm flush to her cheeks. He finished his drink. 'But now we'll eat.'

When they walked into the restaurant, the owner's

wife, slight, dark and bright-eyed, came to welcome them, and there were greetings from everyone in the room as they went to their table.

They began with a creamy vegetable soup. Rohan chose *escargots* as his next course, but Sabine laughingly declined to share them with him.

'I'm not quite French enough — not yet,' she said.

He smiled back at her. 'It will happen.'

Her own *petit friture* was a plateful of tiny fish, crisply fried and sprinkled with garlic, and they both opted for guinea fowl casseroled in red wine, and so tender it almost fell off the bone, with sautéd potatoes and cabbage cooked in butter, as their main course. They drank red wine too from a small earthenware jug, toasting each other, savouring the delectable flavours of the food and their new-found joy.

Sabine thought, I'll remember this meal all my life, from the smallest crumb of bread to the pattern on the china — and how happy we are.

Coffee was brought and a platter of pale, sharp cheeses. They talked about everything and nothing, as they embarked on their mutual voyage of discovery, learning that they both had a passion for reading, and enjoyed the cinema and going to concerts. Both of them skiied, and played tennis, and Rohan, in addition, played rugby each winter, and was dedicated, like most of his fellow-countrymen, to *la chasse*.

'Isn't it amazing that we have so much in common?' she marvelled.

He shook his head. 'What else do you expect — when you meet the other half of yourself?'

She traced a line on the tablecloth with her nail. 'Is that what we've done?' Her voice was shy.

'Yes,' he said. 'And I knew it from that first day when you came driving down to the *chais* like a crazy woman. I think the shock of that recognition drove me a little crazy myself. You—everything about you—presented a complication I didn't need in my life.' He groaned. 'I wanted to seize you in my arms, but at the same time drive you away into oblivion—pretend I'd never seen you—that you didn't exist.' His voice roughened. 'But each time I saw you I could feel myself weakening—wanting to be close to you.'

Sabine smiled impishly. 'I would never have guessed it.'

'I didn't intend you to,' he said with a trace of grimness. He reached across the table and took her hand. 'What do you plan for this afternoon?'

'I need to go and look at this furniture for the house,' she admitted. 'Were you thinking of something else?'

He smiled ruefully. 'I wanted to take you round my vineyard—show you my world, but it can wait.'

Unbidden, Antoinette's angry words came back into her mind, and niggled there.

'They mean everything to you—the vines, don't they?' she said slowly.

'They must—to any *vigneron*. The vines are greedy—hardy, and they push deep roots down into the soil, but they are also vulnerable. They need constant attention, constant vigilance, like a nursery of children. When the vines flower early, the vintage is usually better, but that also brings the danger of a late frost in April killing the buds.

'But every season of the year brings its own hazards,' he added. 'No one has forgotten the devastation that Phylloxera brought to our vineyards. We can't afford another such disaster. It won't happen to my vines.'

The pride of possession in his voice troubled her. La Tour Monchauzet didn't belong to him, after all, but to the *Baron*. She bit her lip. Was it Monsieur de Rochefort who'd tried to persaude Rohan to marry Antoinette? she wondered. And was that the price he'd be expected to pay for his dream?

She looked down at her empty plate, wanting to probe, but reluctant at the same time to seem too inquisitive — to breach, even slightly, the warmth of their newly fledged accord. 'It must be difficult for you — not being completely in charge,' she ventured.

'I hate it,' he said frankly. 'But it won't continue for much longer. I shall make sure of that, with your help.' He threw his head back. 'I'm going to take control — be my own master at last, and to hell with everything else.'

But how? she wanted to ask. And what have I got to do with it?

He pushed back his chair, signalling for the bill. 'Now let's go and look at your furniture.' And the moment was lost.

As she followed him out into the sunshine, Sabine thought, I'll ask him later, and pushed the memory of Antoinette's venom to the furthest recesses of her mind.

It was an idyllic afternoon. Monsieur Pallon was a portly man with a luxuriant moustache and twinkling eyes, and he was clearly delighted at the prospect of having some of the floor space in his depot returned to him. As Mademoiselle Lavaux had said, much of the furniture dated from a different era, and was ornately carved in dark, heavy wood. It was totally different from anything Sabine possessed in England, but that only added to its charm.

She could imagine it all back at Les Hiboux — was already planning out loud where she would place the various pieces, while Rohan and Monsieur Pallon exchanged indulgent glances, and settled the details of how and where it was all to be delivered.

She almost danced back to the car. It seemed impossible that in a few short days her life could have changed so dramatically and fundamentally, and she told Rohan so.

'I was so miserable when I came here, and everyone rejected me all over again,' she said. 'But now I'm really beginning to feel I belong.'

He kissed her, swiftly and fiercely. 'And you always will,' he said. 'I'll see to that.' He reached to the back seat, and handed her a pretty carrier bag. 'This is for you.'

The tissue-wrapped contents proved to be a skirt, romantically full and swirling, and matching low-necked top in a silky print of tiny black and white flowers.

'Oh.' The folds cascaded through her hands on to her lap. 'It's lovely. It's from the shop in the square where they make all the dresses from their own fabrics.' She remembered how much they'd cost too. 'But I — I can't accept it.'

He touched her cheek with his hand. 'Yes, you can,'

he contradicted firmly. 'It's to replace the one I—damaged yesterday.'

'But that can be mended,' she protested, blushing slightly. 'It was only a couple of buttons. . .'

'Then take this as an apology for the inconvenience.' He smiled at her, his eyes dancing wickedly. 'Wear it for me tonight.'

'I can't,' she said, downcast. 'I'm going to have dinner with Mademoiselle Lavaux and Marie-Christine.'

'What a coincidence,' he said softly. 'So is Jacques, and so am I. I hope you don't object. You see, I needed to see you away from the château, and I couldn't be sure you'd come with me today. So I made a contingency plan with Monique's help.'

Sabine laughed as he started the car. 'You're very determined, Monsieur Saint Yves,' she teased. 'And very manipulative.'

'I get what I want,' he nodded, and shot her an unsmiling glance. 'Is that so wrong?'

'I—suppose not.' She found the hint of ruthlessness in his voice vaguely disturbing. It reminded her how little she really knew about him—about his character—his ambitions, and the lengths he might go to achieve them.

She was in love with a man who was still a virtual stranger to her, she thought, and shivered, as if a cloud had passed suddenly across the sun.

CHAPTER EIGHT

THAT vaguely troubled feeling still persisted as Sabine got ready for the dinner party that evening. She had the impression she was on some kind of rollercoaster ride, exhilarating but inherently dangerous.

She thought again, Things don't happen like this— not to people like me. It's all going too far and too fast, and felt a little uneasy *frisson* shiver between her shoulder-blades.

Because by nature she wasn't a risk-taker. Or was she? She hardly knew any more. She'd come to France to find her identity, and the search wasn't over yet. She knew that with total certainty.

The skirt and top Rohan had given her only added to her inner confusion. The style was too extravagant, too romantic when compared with the simple, even tailored clothes she normally chose.

She looked into the mirror, moving her hips in time to some silent music in her head, letting the silky skirt swish enticingly around her legs— And saw another stranger looking back at her, eyes and mouth dreaming and vulnerable.

Turning away hurriedly, she caught sight of the bed, and wondered if she would sleep there alone tonight, or if the choice was even hers to make. She draped a plain white shawl round her shoulders, and walked slowly to the farm.

She received a charming welcome from Monique Lavaux, and a boisterous one from Marie-Christine, who promptly dragged her off to her room to see the wedding dress she was making for herself, in fold after fold of shimmering ivory brocade. It was beautiful, and the work Marie-Christine was putting into it was exquisite, and Sabine told her so sincerely.

'I'm so happy you like it.' Marie-Christine was bubbling. 'You will come to the wedding? Of course you will. I won't take no for an answer.' She lowered her voice. 'Besides, I wish to ask you a big favour.'

'Ask away,' Sabine said, amused.

'We would like to borrow your house — Jacques and I — for our wedding night. It is the custom, you understand, for the bride and groom to slip away from the wedding during the evening celebration, and hide somewhere — at a friend's for example.' She rolled her eyes. 'The better the hiding-place, the more privacy we have before the guests find us.'

'Do they always find you?'

'Oh, yes, eventually,' Marie-Christine said serenely. 'And they bring us the *tourain*.'

Sabine's brow wrinkled. 'I don't think I understand.'

'A big pot of garlic soup,' Marie-Christine explained. 'Very hot with egg in the Périgordine style, and a lot of black pepper.' She grinned. 'This is for the groom.'

'I see,' Sabine commented drily. 'And what happens then?'

'We wash our hands in a basin of water, and we drink the soup. It's a tradition. Only, we don't make it too easy for them to find us.'

'I understand that too. Of course you may borrow the house, and I won't mention it to anyone.'

'Thank you a thousand times.' Marie-Christine gave her an arch look. 'Perhaps in time we can perform a similar service to you.'

'Perhaps.' Sabine tried to sound non-committal and was furious with herself for blushing.

The main living area of the farmhouse was one large room, with a wooden staircase leading off it, and an expensively fitted kitchen at one end, separated by a peninsular unit, behind which Monique was bustling happily.

Rohan and Jacques had arrived when the two girls returned, and were sipping their aperitifs while Monique put the finishing touches to her meal.

'It is only simple,' she apologised as she brought the first course to the table. 'I love to cook, but my work leaves little time.'

'Garlic soup?' Rohan's brows lifted appreciatively as a creamy liquid was ladled into his bowl. 'Isn't this a little premature, Monique?'

She laughed. 'I wanted to give Sabine something typical of the Périgord.'

Marie-Christine caught Sabine's eyes and gave an expressive wink. Sabine sampled the soup, and found the flavour surprisingly delicate. The egg which had been stirred into it gave an unusual texture, and the pepper added pungency. To her surprise both Rohan and Jacques poured red wine into their bowls as they drank, and Marie-Christine explained this was known as *chabrot*.

Smoked duck's breast on a bed of mixed salad came

next, followed by a meaty chicken terrine, cut into thick slices and served alone. The main course was rabbit sautéed quickly with garlic, accompanied by tiny potatoes cooked in their jackets; a bowl of green salad was also passed round.

'And cheese?' Sabine said faintly, soon after, as a platter with several varieties was placed in the middle of the table. 'I won't be able to walk after all this.'

Then, finally, a sponge pudding soaked in liqueur and decorated with fresh pineapple and cherries was served. It occurred to her that if this was a simple meal she would hate to see what Monique Lavaux could do when she was really trying.

With the coffee, Armagnac was offered, and an innocuous-looking local spirit, served in a tall bottle with a carved wooden figure inside it. Sabine, coaxed into taking a sip from Rohan's glass, felt as if the top of her head had exploded, and laughingly refused any more. All during the meal, she'd been aware of his eyes on her across the table, the warmth in them as tangible as a caressing hand. She told herself to be sensible, and concentrate on the food and the others around the table, but all the same she could feel a soft, trembling excitement building inside her.

Conversation during the meal had been general, but now it turned more specifically to the château, and the prospects of the year's vintage. Jacques was speaking enthusiastically about the crop of grapes which the vines had produced, and was prophesying a bumper harvest. The talk quickly became too technical for

Sabine to follow, and Marie-Christine laughed at her
bemused expression.

'Making wine is not just an occupation,' she said. 'It
is a way of life. You will have to accustom yourself to
that,' she added, with a droll wrinkle of her nose.

Sabine felt that betraying flush rise in her cheeks
again. But there was nothing she could say in way of
denial. No one could have misread the significance of
Rohan's attitude to her.

Between them, she and Marie-Christine loaded the
dish-washer, while Monique, with a tolerant eye on the
engrossed pair at the table, made more coffee, before
settling down with her *petit-point*. Sabine welcomed
Marie-Christine's suggestion that they should take their
coffee up to her room, and look at some furniture
catalogues. She needed to get out of Rohan's orbit for
a while — to try and pull herself together, she thought
almost frantically. She was unnerved by her total
awareness of him, and the unaccustomed gnaw of
longing deep within her. Even when she'd been helping
in the kitchen she'd found her eyes straying, as if
magnetised, in his direction. And knew that he knew it
too.

It seemed impossible that she could have fallen in
love so swiftly and completely, especially when she'd
managed to remain heart-whole quite effortlessly all
this time. No other man had ever been able to arouse
more than a tingle of interest in her. Now she felt the
full pulsation of desire throbbing through her body, the
peaks of her untrammelled breasts hardening involun-
tarily against the sweet friction of her silky top.

Safely out of the sight and sound of him, she gazed

raptly at glossy brochures and debated the merits of sofa-beds over plain settees with all the enthusiasm Marie-Christine could have wished. She also had to parry some delighted but pointed questioning about Rohan.

'I'm so happy for you—for both of you,' the other girl confided. 'I've known Rohan a long time, but I've never seen him this way with a woman before, or with such immediacy. A veritable *coup de foudre*, eh?'

Sabine laughed awkwardly. 'Well, yes. It's never happened to me before either.' She hesitated. 'But you suggested that he had Antoinette. . .'

Marie-Christine shrugged largely. 'Oh, well, as to that—it seemed the sensible thing if Rohan wanted to be master of La Tour Monchauzet. And naturally it was the wish of the *Baron* and *madame*. But neither he nor Antoinette are direct blood descendants of Monsieur de Rochefort, so there would have been heavy financial penalties attached to the inheritance.' She smiled archly at Sabine. 'And now you have given his thoughts a different direction anyway, so that solves everything.'

Did it? Sabine wondered as they returned downstairs. If Rohan really wanted control of the vineyard, would he consider it well lost for love once the first passion had cooled, as it inevitably would? At some future time might he blame her for the loss of his dream?

Then she saw him look across at her and smile, and all her uncertainties vanished like morning mist before the sun. For good or ill, she belonged to him, and the future would have to take care of itself.

The sky was thick with stars as they walked down the track towards Les Hiboux. Rohan's arm lay lightly across her shoulders, filling her with a languorous and delicious warmth. When they reached the house, he took the key from her and unlocked the door. Her whole body trembled as he took her in his arms. Her lips parted eagerly to receive his kiss, and she clung to his shoulders as the world quavered and shook around her. He swung her up into his arms and carried her over the threshold into the shadowy interior and beyond to the shuttered darkness of the bedroom.

The bed received her softly. He did not join her immediately as she'd half expected, but sat down beside her. He took her hand, lifting it to his lips, brushing his mouth softly across the palm, until her whole being shivered with the intimacy of the contact. She wanted more, but was unsure how to tell him. Her lack of experience, which had never concerned her before, seemed suddenly grotesque. The ordinary communication of words was inadequate to convey all she was feeling, all that she desired. She was as tongue-tied and gauche as a schoolgirl on a first date.

Shyly, guided by instinct, she put her other hand on the front of his shirt, feeling the warmth of his skin through the smooth, crisp fabric, before releasing one button, then another. Her fingers slid inside, rediscovering the hair-roughened wall of his chest, touching the flat male nipples and feeling them harden beneath her tentative exploration.

He said quietly and very gravely, 'Sabine — are you sure? Because, after tonight, there can be no turning back for either of us.'

She whispered, 'I'm quite sure.'

'So be it, then.'

Sabine could hear the rustle of his clothes as he removed them. Then he lay down beside her, and drew her gently into his arms. For a moment, she was tense when she felt the strength and power of his naked body against her own, but there was no pressure, no instant demand in his embrace, and she soon relaxed again. He began to touch her very lightly, his hand stroking her face, the curve of her throat, and the cool skin exposed by the low neck of her top.

He said softly, 'You looked very beautiful tonight. This——' his fingers brushed the flimsy fabric where it stretched over her breasts and lingered '—this was a great success.'

'You—you have very good taste.' Her own voice was husky. 'It's a—lovely outfit.'

'I hoped you would like it. But it would be a pity to allow it to crease, don't you think?' He paused interrogatively. 'Well?'

'I—suppose so,' she managed at last, dry-mouthed.

Without fumbling or undue haste, Rohan freed her from the silky folds. The night air felt suddenly cool on her uncovered body, and she shivered. He lifted himself on to one elbow and looked down at her. 'Is this the first time?'

'That I've let a man undress me?' Sabine prevaricated.

'Not just that.' Faint laughter stirred in his voice. 'Anything with a man.'

'Is it so obvious?' she asked in a low voice. She hesitated. 'Are—are you disappointed?'

'No,' he said. 'I am overwhelmed. I don't deserve such an exquisite gift.'

The breath caught in her throat as his hands cupped her naked breasts, his thumbs stroking the already erect nipples, making them throb with a pleasure that was akin to anguish. She let her head fall back on the pillow, her body arching in swift sensuousness, inviting and inciting the continuation of his caresses.

He bent his head, letting his mouth take possession of first one eager, engorged peak, then the other, suckling them gently and luxuriously, making her gasp and writhe beneath him, her body blooming with a faint film of perspiration. Her hands lifted to cradle his head, and hold him against her, her fingers raking through the crisp dark hair. She found herself savouring almost frantically the strangeness, the rightness of it all, felt the silent, urgent clamour of her body as it pressed against his, wanting more — always more. . .

'Patience,' he whispered against her skin. 'We have all night, my heart, my beautiful one.'

He let the tip of his tongue traverse the valley between her breasts, and continue down over the sensitive midriff to the taut hollow of her belly. At the same time, his hand slid gently from her shoulder to the curve of her hip, soothing her as if she was some young and frightened animal — as perhaps she was — and paused, one finger outlining, almost idly, the concealing lacy triangle of her briefs. A new stark tension gripped her. She was rigid, every sense alerted, waiting suddenly. . . His hand repeated the movement, coaxingly, begulingly.

Sabine realised she had almost stopped breathing.

His hand moved again, found her, touched her with a knowledge older than the world, making her whole being convulse in sudden startled pleasure. Her throat constricted in a soundless, wordless moan, and he bent and touched his mouth to hers, the tip of his tongue meeting hers lightly, teasingly, mirroring the silken play of his fingers.

One incredible sensation seemed to pursue another through her consciousness. She realised somehow that she was completely naked now, every secret of her womanhood surrendered to the honeyed eroticism of his caresses. For the first time in her life, she was discovering exactly what level of response her untutored and bewildered body might be capable of. Limbs pliant, reason suspended, she lay in a universe where nothing mattered except that he should not stop.

His lips travelled to her ear, probing the tiny sensitive whorls, then took a leisurely path down her throat to her breasts, toying with her ardently expectant nipples, before moving without haste down her body. And down.

'Ah, God.' The sound was torn out of her. 'No — you can't. . .' But even as she spoke her body was twisting, lifting almost of its own volition, offering itself to this new intimacy in greedy delight. Wave after wave of a pleasure bordering on exaltation raised her gently to some peak, ebbed a little, then carried her up again, more fiercely than before. She was the tide, and Rohan her inexorable moon, beckoning her without mercy to some unknown strand.

When at last he allowed the wave to break, she broke with it, mind and body shattering, fragmenting

in rapture. She could hear herself sobbing, experienced
the scalding release of tears on her fevered face. Rohan
cradled her in his arms, murmuring to her, soothing
her, praising her. He made her close her eyes, rest for
a while, her head pillowed on his shoulder. She slept a
little—perhaps he did too—then woke once more to
the warm arousal of his kiss, the murmur of his voice
against her ear, summoning her to another feast of
delight.

He encouraged her to explore his body in turn, to use
the same delicate, sensual curiosity he had shown her.
She was shy at first, scared of failing him, but his
undisguised pleasure in her tentative caresses made her
gain confidence, and become bolder. He made her
sharply and joyously aware that he wanted her not as a
submissive toy, but as a full partner in their lovemaking,
sharing the same ardour, the same urgency. Her hands
became eager, demanding on his body, as the sweet, hot
spiral of need began to build in her again.

When, at last, he lifted himself over her, she was
more than ready, welcoming him into her with a little
whimper of bliss. It was all so simple, she found herself
thinking, as coherent thought faded before the renewed
onslaught of sensation. All so wonderfully, ecstatically
simple. And complex. And complete.

She clung to him, their mouths drinking hectically
from one another, their harsh breathing mingled;
moved with him, her slim legs clamped round his waist,
climbed with him higher and higher into some fierce
and unimagined realm of pleasure.

Suddenly, they were at the world's end, her body
convulsing in astonished and savage joy, as she heard

him cry out hoarsely in his own release. Afterwards, they lay quietly together, wrapped in each other's arms, smiling a little, totally at peace.

She said, 'I didn't know it could be like that.'

'Nor I.' Gently Rohan smoothed the sweat-dampened hair back from her forehead.

'But it wasn't — the first time — for you. It couldn't have been.' Contemplating the others who might have shared this infinity of delight with him was like probing an open wound.

'It was the first time with the woman I love.' He touched her mouth softly with his own. 'That is all that matters. The past doesn't count any more. There is only the future — our future.'

There was an odd vehemence in his tone. Sabine stared up at him.

'You really think it can be that easy?'

'I shall make it so,' he said with a touch of grimness. 'Trust me.' He kissed her again. 'Now let's get some sleep.'

She felt hollow, light-headed with happy weariness, but sleep was strangely elusive just the same. But it was good just to lie in the darkness, curled against him, listening to his even breathing, and know this was just the first night of the rest of their lives.

Somewhere in the stillness of the night an owl hooted — the first one she'd heard since she came to live at Les Hiboux, Sabine realised, surprised.

So much for the bird of ill-omen, she thought drowsily. With Rohan's arms round her, nothing could harm her now.

* * *

The next time she opened her eyes, she was alone in the big bed. In the distance, she could hear the splash of the shower, and the fragrance of coffee hung tantalisingly in the air.

Sabine sat up, shivered a little in the cool of the early morning air, as Rohan walked in, a towel knotted round his hips, carrying two cups.

'Do you have to go?' She watched in disappointment as he reached for his clothes.

'Of course.' He slanted a sardonic brow at her. 'A *vigneron's* day begins early, my love. As it is, I've stayed longer than I intended.' He finished his coffee, and knelt on the bed to kiss her deeply and lingeringly. 'I'll see you at the château tonight for dinner.' He paused. 'You hadn't forgotten you were invited?'

'No, of course not, but can't — won't I see you before that?'

'So greedy?' he teased, caressing one pink-tipped breast.

'I didn't think I was,' she said wryly, and he laughed.

'I'm flattered, but it's better that we wait until tonight, believe me. Quite apart from the vines, I have a heavy day ahead of me — a lot of serious talking to do. Matters that affect us both.'

'Such as?' She frowned a little.

'I'll explain everything tonight,' he said. He touched her cheek. 'Don't worry about it. You have a busy day too, remember. Monsieur Pallon is bringing your furniture.'

'So he is,' she said slowly. The laughter had gone from Rohan's face. He was preoccupied suddenly, at a distance from her, and she wanted him back. She needed the new-found intimacy of the night translated into daytime terms.

At the same time, she recognised she was being unreasonable. Their commitment to each other was made, after all, and she couldn't expect Rohan to jettison every other aspect of his life in her favour.

She looked up at him, forcing a smile. 'Off you go, then, and I'll — see you tonight.'

'Yes.' He took one last kiss, frowning slightly. 'We'll spend the whole of tomorrow together, I promise.'

Reluctantly Sabine unclasped her arms from his neck. 'I'll cook you a meal.' She grinned at him. 'Something English.'

She slipped on a robe and went to the door to wave goodbye to him. It was a grey morning, she thought with a shiver, the sky heavily overcast with cloud which had appeared out of nowhere during one night. But at least it would be cooler for shifting furniture around.

By the time Monsieur Pallon's van arrived, it was raining, and the delivery of the furniture took place almost on the run. Sabine concentrated solely on making sure the appropriate pieces got into the right rooms. The fun of choosing the exact position for each item, and making the final adjustments, could wait until she was on her own.

It was mid-afternoon before she had Les Hiboux sorted to her approximate satisfaction. She was clammy with sweat, and her arms and shoulders ached with tugging and heaving. Old Hercule's stuff had been built to last, she reflected ruefully as she turned on the shower.

She dressed in clean jeans and a shirt, and drove to

Villereal to shop for the following day. It was still raining, and the washed and windless air, such a contrast to the heat of the previous days, struck a distinct chill as she dashed to the Intermarché. She'd already decided what she was going to cook for Rohan—home-made tomato soup to begin with, then *le rosbif* with all the trimmings, although she was going to cheat on the dessert and buy one of the beautifully glazed *tartes aux pommes* from a *pâtisserie*.

As she drove back, she reviewed her scanty wardrobe in her mind's eyes, wondering what would be appropriate for dinner at the *château*. Whatever she chose, it couldn't compete with the couturier clothes worn by the *Baronne* or Antoinette, she thought with a grimace.

Not that any amount of designer labels would or could reconcile her to the prospect of meeting Antoinette again. She was frankly dreading any further confrontation with the other girl. Unlike Rohan, she wasn't convinced that Antoinette could be so easily dismissed from their lives. It was something they needed to talk about. It was, maybe, one of the serious topics that Rohan was already discussing today, trying to smooth the path to her recognition as his future wife.

She still found it hard to assimilate the way her life had changed so drastically in the course of a mere few days. She'd come to investigate the past, and discovered her own future instead.

She parked the car and hoisted the plastic carriers from the boot, perching the flat, be-ribboned *pâtisserie* box on top. She saw the note as soon as she got to the door. It had been left on the terrace this time, anchored down by a stone. No envelope either, just a slip of paper, folded in two, containing a brief typewritten message. 'I must talk to you before tonight. Meet me at the tower at five o'clock. R.'

She gave herself a small mental hug. It was just what she needed — to see him, to have the reassurance of him before she faced the evening at the château.

Not that the wording of the message was particularly reassuring, she admitted, as she put her provisions away. Perhaps there'd been some trouble — some kind of scene he wanted to warn her about. If so, she would simply invent a diplomatic headache, and stay away from La Tour Monchauzet altogether. She'd suffered enough traumas and indignities already, she thought grimly.

The rain had subsided by the time she was ready to set out, so she only needed to knot a sweater round her shoulders. But the woods were dank and damp, and every icy, unexpected drip on to her hair or down the back of her neck made her regret having left her umbrella behind long before she reached the tower.

She was early for their rendezvous, but Rohan had still arrived before her, apparently, because the massive door was slightly open. She squeezed round it and called to him, but there was no answer, and she frowned a little, as she stood looking round her. She'd been so sure she would find him there. . .

It occurred to her suddenly that she found the cloak-and-dagger element in all this vaguely disturbing, and totally unnecessary. If Rohan needed to have a private word with her, why hadn't he arranged to see her at the house instead? For one thing, it would have been warmer, she thought, wriggling her shoulders defensively and wishing she'd brought a jacket. The interior of the tower was like a refrigerator. Maybe Rohan had thought so too, and gone for a walk, rather than hang around waiting, and getting frozen.

And there was still something about the place's atmosphere that she found unnerving. It was the last place in the world she would ever have chosen for a tryst, as she would tell him when he turned up.

She untied the sleeves of her sweater and began to pull it on over her head, aware as she did so of a faint muffled sound behind her. She emerged from the confines of the turtle-neck, and turned quickly, shaking her hair into place, her lips parting in a smile—— And stopped right there. Because the noise she'd heard wasn't Rohan's arrival at all. It had been the door swinging shut behind her, closing her alone into this claustrophobic space.

And as her stomach muscles constricted, and her throat tightened in swift, unsteading alarm, she heard the unmistakable grating of a key in the huge lock.

She was a prisoner.

CHAPTER NINE

THE important thing, of course, was not to panic. This was clearly a very bad joke, by some misguided person, or it was a mistake. Someone had seen the open door, and fastened it up in a fit of misplaced zeal. Either way, having hysterics wouldn't help.

Sabine decided to take several slow, deep breaths instead. Then she walked to the door, and tried to open it, just in case the sound of the key had been a figment of her over-active imagination. But the huge timbers refused to budge. She took another breath and yelled, 'Hi, there!' at the top of her voice, banging on the door with both fists as she did so— And heard the sound die away into a profound and unresponsive silence. Whoever had shut the door had gone.

Sucking bruised knuckles, she retired to the sagging sofa, and tried to think. It had to be a mistake, she thought. Only Rohan, after all, knew of their meeting, and crude practical jokes just weren't his style. So she was a victim of understandable human error. The tower was off limits, after all, and someone was just ensuring that the *Baron's* orders were carried out to the letter.

All well and good. Because there was really nothing to worry about. Any moment now, Rohan would be arriving to keep their appointment, and her problem would be over.

Restlessly, she glanced at her watch. Any moment now. . .

An hour later, she'd stopped thinking in those precise terms, and was trying to tell herself he'd been detained. A phone call, she thought, or some visitor. Anything could have happened. She shivered. It was a long way to sunset, but the air in the tower seemed to be getting colder by the moment. She was becoming bitterly uncomfortable.

She wished she'd brought the note with her. She was beginning to wonder if she'd misread it—got the time all wrong. Yet the couple of typewritten lines had been plain enough, with little room for error.

Her train of thought stopped right there, and she sat up suddenly, as a number of things occurred to her all at once. Firstly, how could she be sure that note had actually come from Rohan? Anyone could have typed that message and his initial, she realised with dismay. In fact, she wasn't even sure she'd told Rohan she knew where the tower was located, let alone that she'd been there. All she'd done was show him that photograph of Fabien, she remembered restively.

No one knew she'd actually been here—except possibly. . .

She paused. '*Isabelle's daughter*'. The recollection of those whispered words came rushing back to haunt her. Except—someone who might have watched her—followed her. . .

Sabine bit her lip, sinking her teeth into the soft inner flesh. It wasn't the kind of possibility she wanted to contemplate, she told herself firmly. She was being melodramatic. Allowing her imagination to run away with her again. There had to be a perfectly simple explanation to all this — if only she could think what it was.

In spite of everything, her mind kept returning to Antoinette — seeing her face as it had been during their last confrontation in Monpazier, twisted with bitterness and hate. It was not a memory she cherished. But was the other girl really capable of this kind of spite? And, if so, what did she hope to gain by it?

Because I'll be found — sooner or later, Sabine thought. I may be hungry, thirsty and chilly, but I'll be found. And then she'll have some explaining to do. Only that wasn't much consolation at the moment, she admitted, as she began to walk up and down, flapping her arms to drive away the permeating cold.

Hungry, she thought, suddenly. Of course. That was her salvation. When she didn't arrive for dinner at the château, they would institute a search. And someone would think of the tower — eventually.

The problem was making her presence known to any search party. The walls and door were so thick that she wasn't sure her cries would be heard. And the windows on the ground floor at least were too high to reach, otherwise she could have sacrificed her sweater to hang out like a flag of distress. Except she'd probably freeze without it.

Time crawled past. She could tell by the angle of the light that it would soon be sunset, and the prospect of being here in the dark appalled her. Already, she'd heard all kinds of rustlings and scufflings from the floor above. Little as she relished the idea, she supposed she would have to go up there before the light went altogether — see if there was some kind of signal she could make to advertise her presence.

She went up the narrow stone stairs with infinite care, reflecting that the last thing she needed was to slip and sprain something, and peered cautiously around her. A bird, a pigeon perhaps, took startled flight, its wings almost brushing her, and Sabine jumped back against the wall, her heart hammering.

The floorboards in the centre of the room had clearly rotted, leaving gaping holes in places, and she edged her way round the perimeter, keeping the wall at her back all the time. The windows up here were waist-high, but very deep, and she found that by lifting herself up into the actual narrow embrasure, and leaning precariously forward, she could get a limited view of the clearing below. But it appeared totally deserted, she acknowledged with a sigh. Devoid of either anxious friends, or triumphant adversaries. As she was about to wriggle back into the room, the faint scent of the climbing rose came to her nostrils, and she sniffed it appreciatively, then paused, remembering the legend. It had worked for that other Sabine, she thought. So it was worth a try, at least.

She took a deep breath and leaned out further, groping for the nearest bloom, closing her eyes to the drop beneath her. The rose didn't give up without a struggle. It had thorns like daggers, Sabine discovered, wincing with the pain of her torn fingers. Well, if all else failed, she could always bleed out of the window, she thought, with a mordant shrug.

Eventually she managed to pick three blooms. She held them for a moment, inhaling their perfume. She whispered, 'Help him to find me — please,' then threw them down, one at a time, into the gathering shadows. It was impossible to see where they'd landed, so all she could do was hope.

She retreated back downstairs, and climbed on to the mildewed sofa, hugging her knees up to her chin. And waited.

In spite of her discomfort, she must have dozed off, because she found herself sitting up with a start, all her senses suddenly alerted by the sound of a key, the creak of a hinge. Her throat constricted in passionate relief. Rohan had come. She'd been found at last.

She began to say, 'Thank God. . .' then halted, as the door swung open and she saw a figure momentarily silhouetted against the pale evening light. Into the shadows of the room came the beam of a powerful flashlight, and she flung up a hand to shield her eyes from its glare.

But the shaft of light didn't waver. It stayed on her, pinning her down mercilessly, like a fly trapped in amber. And from somewhere behind it she heard once more the menacing whisper, 'Isabelle's daughter.'

Only this time she recognised the voice.

She uncurled herself, and got to her feet, grimacing slightly at the pain in her cramped muscles. She said quietly, 'Good evening, *Madame la Baronne*. May I ask the meaning of all this?'

There was a silence, then Héloise de Rochefort said, her voice grating, 'You cannot stay here. You should never have come. You must go away — to England — tonight.'

'Why should I do that?' Sabine kept her own tone level.

'Because you're not wanted here.' The intensity deepened in the old woman's voice. 'When you came, you ruined everything. The same story repeated all over again. I saw the way Rohan looked at you. I knew what it meant. You had come — Isabelle's daughter — to steal another woman's man, as your mother did before you.' She gave a little harsh laugh.

'I followed you both the way I used to do so many years ago. I saw you together. But I won't allow you to take Rohan. I stopped your mother all those years ago, and I shall stop you now.'

Sabine was very still. She said quietly, 'What do you mean?'

'Antoinette is to marry Rohan. It's what I planned for her — what I've dreamed of for her all these years. Nothing and no one is going to get in the way of that dream. We had no children of our own,' the *Baronne* almost choked on the words, 'but there was always Antoinette, my beautiful, radiant Antoinette, dearer to me than any daughter could have been. Rohan belongs to her. So does the vineyard — everything. Gaston was on the point of making her his heir. Until you came.' She drew a hissing breath.

'When I saw you at the side of the road, it was as if a nightmare had come true. For a moment — ah, *Dieu!* — I thought it was Isabelle herself, who had dared to return.'

It was eerie listening to this voice, one moment high and hysterical, sibilant as a snake's the next, issuing from the shadows as if directed down that merciless beam of light. Sabine could see the *Baronne's* figure, rigid and unyielding, blocking the doorway. But for the heavy torch in the older woman's hand she might have been tempted to make a dash for it. In the circumstances, she supposed wryly, it was safer to stay where she was. It was also important to remain calm, and not reveal how unnerving she found this confrontation.

She said quietly, 'It's no business of mine who inherits La Tour Monchauzet, *madame*, unless you think I have some prior claim through Monsieur Fabien. But I swear to you that's not something I intend to pursue.'

The *Baronne* laughed harshly. 'Are you really still so naïve, *mademoiselle*? Even if you genuinely wished to forgo your claim, do you think Rohan would allow it? What a romantic notion you must have of him.'

'We've fallen in love with each other,' Sabine said quietly. 'It wasn't something either of us expected, perhaps. . .'

'Oh, there was no question that Rohan would want you—once he realised who you were. And he knows. He had an interview with my husband this afternoon. I listened at the door. He knows everything.'

'Then he's much wiser than I am,' Sabine returned wearily. 'I don't understand any of this.' She took a deep breath. 'However, you must be aware, *madame*, that Rohan has never—cared for Antoinette in that way. You can't want her to marry someone who doesn't love her in return.'

'She wants him. That is enough. Sometimes in life it has to be enough.' The *Baronne's* voice was brittle. 'And Rohan has always wanted La Tour Monchauzet.

He would have taken her to make it his own, just as he is now taking you.'

Sabine's head lifted sharply. 'What do you mean?'

'Are you really such a fool? Of course, with you he has to pretend — to play the lover. He was with you last night, wasn't he? I saw him return this morning, so pleased with himself.'

Warm blood stung Sabine's face. 'I think that's our business.'

'Oh, yes,' the *Baronne* said bitterly. 'With Rohan, it is always a matter of business. Or did he really make you believe he had developed some sudden, over-whelming passion for you?'

It was like being on stage in a spotlight, which revealed every minor action and reaction. Sabine did her best not to flinch from the contempt in *madame's* voice as well as the implications of what she was saying. But there was a sour taste in her throat suddenly. She thought, I don't want to hear any more of this. Aloud, she said coolly, 'I don't think this conversation is getting us anywhere, *madame*. And I'm still waiting for you to explain why you locked me in here.'

'So that you would go, just as she did, and never come back.' The older woman's tone was almost matter-of-fact.

Sabine caught her breath. 'Are you saying you locked my mother in here?' she demanded.

She saw the poised head nod slightly. 'Of course. But in her case I was able to leave her in here much longer. Fabien was away, and Gaston had gone to Bordeaux on business, so there was no one to raise the alarm.'

She paused. 'I talked to her through the door. I told her that I wouldn't allow her to take him from me. That I would do anything — anything to keep him.' Her voice deepened in intensity for a moment, then became reflective. 'At first, she argued. She didn't realise, you see, that I had followed them, that I had seen them here together — and knew what they were planning.

'She was frightened then, and so, in the end, she agreed to do what I wanted, and leave La Tour Monchauzet forever.'

She's mad. The chilling thought struck Sabine to the bone. She said carefully, 'You — wanted Fabien yourself, *madame*?'

The torch beam jerked suddenly as the *Baronne* moved her hand in an irritable gesture of negation.

'Fabien? What foolishness is this? It was never Fabien. That was just a pretence to cover up her real *affaire*. No, Isabelle's lover was Gaston — my husband. And he was the father of her bastard child.'

Sabine's gasp seemed torn out of her throat. 'No, it can't be true.'

'Ah, but it is,' Rohan said quietly. 'Your father is waiting at the château to greet you as his daughter, Sabine.'

Neither of them had heard his approach. The *Baronne* cried out hoarsely, and turned, the beam of light dipping and wavering like some live and frightened creature seeking sanctuary, as Rohan took the torch from her hand. He said very gently, 'It's all over, Tante Héloïse. There's nothing more you can do.' He called over his shoulder, 'Jacques — come and help *madame*.'

Héloïse de Rochefort stood very still for a moment,

then she covered her face with her hands and began to cry in great, gusty, choking sobs. It was one of the worst sounds Sabine had ever heard.

Jacques appeared in the doorway. He said respectfully, '*Madame*,' and offered her his arm. 'You should go home and rest a little now. Ernestine — everyone has been concerned about you.'

For a moment it seemed as if she would pull away from him, then she nodded, and, still weeping, allowed herself to be led away.

Rohan came to Sabine's side. 'You're all right.' It was a statement rather than a question.

'I — suppose so.' Her voice sounded strained. 'I just feel — stunned — and so terribly cold.'

He slipped off his jacket and put it round her shoulders. 'I did not want you to find out like this,' he said, more gently. 'I planned to tell you myself.' He paused. 'How did she get you here?'

'I found a note at the house. I thought it was from you.' She drew a shuddering breath. 'She locked my mother in here years ago — threatened her. That's why she ran away.'

'It wasn't just that. There were other factors. The child she was having, for example. Obviously, she could not bear to hurt Fabien with the truth.'

Her lips felt stiff. 'How — how long have you known — that the *Baron* was my father?'

'I knew for certain when you showed me that photograph, and I realised it was Gaston, not Fabien whose picture she had kept all those years. This afternoon I confronted him with my suspicions, and he admitted everything. I think it was almost a relief to him — after all this time.' He was silent for a moment. 'It is a painful story. Some aspects of it may shock you.'

'I don't think I can handle any more shocks,' she said with taut bitterness. 'It's bad enough just knowing that Isabelle was having an affair with a married man while she was supposed to be engaged to his brother. I feel as if the woman I loved and looked up to never existed.'

'Talk to your father before you judge her too harshly,' he said.

'Do I have to? I feel as if I just want to leave this place — and never see it — or anyone here ever again.' She didn't look at him as she said this.

'I'm afraid it is essential,' he said. 'You were the one after all who wanted the truth. You can't avoid it now, even if it isn't the clean, pure vindication that you desired.'

'No.' She fought down a sob. 'How — how did you know where to find me?'

'I was on my way down to Les Hiboux when I saw a light in the trees. Jacques caught up with me to say that Tante Héloïse, who'd gone to her room with a supposed migraine, had disappeared too, and Ernestine was having hysterics.' He paused. 'Then I saw these.'

For the first time, she saw he was holding the roses she'd thrown from the window, and he handed them to her. She looked down at them expressionlessly. They were crushed — almost lifeless, but the thorns were still sharp.

As he turned to close the door of the tower behind them, she let them fall to the ground again. The legend—the romantic flight of fancy was over. Her head throbbed as she walked beside him up to the château, and she was fighting a churning nausea deep within her. It wasn't the truth awaiting her at the château that she feared, but one much closer to home. She was Gaston de Rochefort's daughter, and Rohan knew this—had known it when he became her lover; had known it when they began to plan their lives together.

The *Baronne's* words came stinging back at her: 'With Rohan, it is always a matter of business.'

He wanted La Tour Monchauzet. Had wanted it all his life. 'That's what counts with Rohan—the vines'. Anotinette had told her so that day in Monpazier. The day she'd shown him the photograph. . .

But I didn't listen to her, she thought. Because I didn't want to hear. I preferred to think she was just a jealous bitch. I wanted to believe that this man—this stranger—had seen me and wanted me. I needed my own fairy-tale—my own legend—and to see it come true. *And they both lived happily ever after.*

Her throat constricted sharply. She wanted to scream out loud, to strike at him with her fists for destroying her dream. The nails scored the palms of her hands as she fought for control.

Because he wouldn't understand, she thought. He would think she was being totally unreasonable. The French were a practical nation. they knew the value of land—of inheritance. They made arrangements accordingly. She was—part of an arrangement. The plan had been originally for Rohan to marry Antoinette, but because she was the *Baronne's* niece, not Gaston's, the inheritance would have been penalised financially by the government. A daughter—even an illegitimate one—was a much better bargain. And if she was naïve enough to fall in love with him—so much the better. That way he got it all. And she'd been too stupid, too besotted to realise—until now.

There were tears inside her, aching inside her chest, scalding her throat, burning behind her eyes, but she couldn't shed them yet. This was a separate—a private nightmare. The one awaiting her at the château was far more public, and that was the one she had to face head-on.

Every light seemed to be glaring from the windows when they arrived. Rohan took her to a *salon* on the ground floor. The scene that confronted her was like a tableau from a waxworks, she thought with faint hysteria as she walked in.

Héloise de Rochefort was crouched in a chair like a small hunted animal. On one side of her, Antoinette stood like a statue. On the other, Ernestine kept up a flow of low-voiced chatter, permeated by sobs. Gaston de Rochefort sat in his wheelchair by the fireplace. Logs had been kindled in the hearth, and the room held the faint, acrid tang of woodsmoke.

If she could, Sabine would have turned and run, but Rohan's hand was on her shoulder, urging her forward gently but firmly.

'My child.' Gaston's voice throbbed with emotion. 'My girl.' His hands gripped the arms of his chair, levering himself upwards, his face grim and set with determination. As the room fell suddenly, tensely silent, he began to walk, to hobble painfully and with difficulty towards Sabine.

Héloise de Rochefort cried out, and covered her mouth with her hand.

'Oh, God.' Sabine swung on Rohan. 'Help him. Stop him — he'll fall — injure himself.'

'No.' Rohan shook his head, an odd smile playing about his mouth. 'That chair was his refuge, his excuse for avoiding life. It has been for years. But it needed the right impetus to get him out of it. You've supplied that, Sabine. He's going to be fine now.'

Gaston de Rochefort was panting, his forehead heavily beaded with sweat when he reached her. But the arms which seized and held Sabine were strong with no sign of weakness. There were tears in his eyes.

'Little one.' He almost groaned the words. 'If I had only known — if only Isabelle could have forced herself to tell me.'

Sabine heard Madame de Rochefort moan faintly.

'I don't understand.' Her voice shook slightly. 'If — if you were having an affair — you would surely have realised — she would have said something.'

'No.' Gaston closed his eyes, as if wincing away from some unbearable memory. 'It was not like that. There was — no affair.' He paused, drawing breath with an effort. 'May we — sit down?'

Rohan took his arm and guided him to a sofa. Sabine sat down beside him, both her hands clasped in his. The room was warm, but she felt cold, as her father's eyes sadly searched her face.

'This is not easy for me,' he said, after a pause. 'I have to speak of things I wished so often to forget — of

my guilt, of my shame.' He bit his lips. 'I loved your
mother always, I think. Even when I was a child I was
entranced by her. Fabien also, of course, but it was
always me that she seemed to prefer—or so I liked to
think. My parents were concerned at our attachment
to her, although they could understand it. She was
beautiful, good and innocent too, a wife any man
would have been proud of—unless, of course, he was
a de Rochefort of La Tour Monchauzet. Fabien and I
were expected to marry—well. The daughter of our
maître de chai was not considered in any way suitable.
Therefore, as soon as Isabelle was old enough, it was
decided to exploit her aptitude for art by sending her
to Paris—out of harm's way.'

He paused again. 'My father arranged with Hercule
to pay for her training. They were in total agreement
that it was the best thing for both sides that Isabelle
should go. It was seen as an act of prudence. But I
never forgot her—and nor did Fabien.

'Time passed, Hercule became ill, and she returned.
Both Fabien and I had become older, harder, perhaps,
but she had not changed at all. From the moment I saw
her, I knew that I still loved her, and that her absence
had only deepened my passion.'

There was another small stifled sound from the
Baronne.

He went on as if he'd heard nothing. 'It wasn't long
before I realised that Fabien felt the same too. And
he, as a widower, was free to woo her, to offer himself
as her husband. I was—insanely jealous. I arranged to
see Isabelle alone and told her of my feelings.

'She was deeply shocked, and very angry. She

reminded me that I was a married man—forbade me to approach her or speak to her again in that way, but at the same time I knew I had made her think about the old days—the attraction we'd had for each other which she could not deny. I'd made her question her own heart.'

He shook his head, his mouth twisted. 'Dear God, after that, it was like a siege. I would not leave her alone. I told myself that I could not—that I had to make her admit what we both knew—that she was in love with me, and always had been.

'I persuaded her once or twice to meet me at the ruined tower. It had always been our special place from childhood. She was always reluctant, and always implacable. I had a wife. I should not be pressuring her in this way. She begged me in tears to leave her alone—to give her some peace.'

'Do you think I'm a fool? That we're all fools?' Héloise de Rochefort's voice was hoarse—cracked. 'She was your mistress. Your slut.'

Gaston shook his head. 'You were wrong, my poor Héloise. Isabelle was guiltless. I was to blame for everything. Even when it was announced that she and Fabien had become formally engaged I would not give up my pursuit of her. She had been living here at the château, helping with the children, but she moved down to Les Hiboux to get away from me. I knew it was because she was afraid—not just of me, but her own emotions.

'The old attraction couldn't be banished so easily. Their wedding was getting closer all the time. I was half crazy with desire for her—terrified of losing her forever. I begged her to meet me one last time at the tower.' He paused again. 'It was then I told her I would divorce my wife and marry her.'

The room was hushed. His words fell into the silence like stones. The Baronne moved once, convulsively, on her chair, then was still again.

Gaston went on heavily, 'I told her I knew she was in love with me. She did not deny it. She called it infatuation — an illusion which could destroy us both. She said that she loved Fabien, and wanted to be his wife, and build a future with him. She told me, as she'd done so many times, that happiness could never be created out of the misery of other people, that Héloise was already jealous of her and unhappy because of her influence with the children.'

'I hated her,' the *Baronne* said. 'Even my Antoinette was turning to her rather than me. The doctors told me I would never have a child of my own. Antoinette was all I had, and I loved her as if she were my own. She had to love me best in return — only there was always — always Isabelle.' Her voice rose slightly. 'She had stolen my husband. I wasn't going to let her take Antoinette too.'

She looked up at the girl beside her. Antoinette was very pale, with a muscle flickering in her throat, but when her aunt took her hand she didn't pull away.

After a silence, Héloise went on, 'I knew Gaston was tired of me — that he wanted to end our marriage — and I couldn't bear it. He even gave her this.' She tugged the silver medallion from her dress. 'But as he loved her I loved him. I would have done anything to keep him — anything. . .'

'There was no need.' The *Baron's* voice was very gentle. 'She rejected me totally.' His voice cracked slightly. 'She said she had known for some time that she and Fabien could not remain at La Tour Monchauzet after their marriage — that they had been talking together about moving away — of going, perhaps, as far as Australia or California and starting a totally new life. One of the reasons for Fabien's trip was to investigate various possibilities.'

His voice sank almost to a whisper. 'I went a little mad, I think. All those years of wanting her, and for nothing. My love — my name thrown back in my face. I'd always respected her — kept my distance — until then. . .'

He threw his head back, staring straight ahead of him, his eyes filled with agony. He said quietly, 'I took her — I — forced her. She was weeping, pleading, fighting me, but I was obsessed by my own need. I was strong, very strong then. She was going to be Fabien's wife, but I would have her first. I could think of nothing else. Cared for nothing else.' A shudder ran through his entire frame, and he was silent.

Sabine freed her hands from his, staring at him almost dazedly. She said in a low voice, 'You loved her — and yet you did — that? How could you?'

'It's beyond belief, I admit, but it's true, to my eternal sorrow and shame. It was my first and only time with Isabelle, and the memory of it has been a shadow across the whole of my life.' A sigh was torn from him. 'Afterwards — she would not look at me or speak for a long time. At last, all she would say was, "Fabien must not know. He must never know".'

He shook his head. 'I never saw her alone again, although I tried desperately. I thought that now she belonged to me, she could not marry Fabien.' He gave a bitter laugh. 'And I was right. But I did not foresee that she would run away from us both — that we would both lose her forever.' He turned and looked at the slender woman cowering in her chair. There was compassion in his face. 'At least I now know why she ran away.'

He sat up, squaring his shoulders. 'She took the secret of our child with her. She couldn't bear any more — the guilt, the hostility, the confusion, and, of course, the inevitable breach between Fabien and myself when the truth emerged.

'My poor wife's attempt to scare her into flight must have been the final straw. To go — to disappear without trace must have seemed the ideal — the only solution.'

He sighed. 'Then Fabien returned. He was devastated, naturally. He was also suspicious. He asked questions that I didn't want to hear. Accused me of things I didn't want to face. Dragged answers from me that I didn't want to give.' He closed his eyes for a moment. 'Our quarrel was terrible — irrevocable. I still bear the scars of his disgust — his rage.' He shook his head. 'For a moment I thought he was going to kill me. In a way I wish he had done. Because the ultimate penalty was much worse.

'He condemned me to a kind of living death with my guilt — my shame. My life became a torment. I drank too much — rode too hard — took too many risks. That's how I ended up in that chair.

'But even then Fabien never spoke to me again in his lifetime. He made it clear that he stayed at La Tour

Monchauzet because the vines needed him—and because he was sure that one day—somehow—Isabelle would return to him, and he had to be here—waiting.'

He looked at Sabine, his face serious, his eyes almost pleading. 'Can you forgive me, my child? Or will you also turn your back and walk away, condemning me to an eternity of silence?'

Sabine stared down at her hands, locked together in her lap. She was wretchedly conscious of Rohan watching her, his brows drawn together in frowning concentration.

She said quietly, 'No. I can't do that. There's been altogether too much guilt—too much pain already. I'm not prepared to inflict additional suffering——' she glanced across at Madame de Rochefort '—on anyone.'

'You shouldn't have come here.' The *Baronne's* voice was a sudden wail. 'It was all right until you came.'

Her husband gave a tired sigh. 'No, *ma chère*, it has never been all right. But now, maybe, we all get a second chance. The wounds can begin to heal, *hein*?' He took one of Sabine's rigid hands, gently unclenching her fingers. 'Tomorrow, I shall send for the *notaire*, and arrange to formally acknowledge you as my only child.'

Sabine bit her lower lip until she tasted blood. 'Is that really necessary? Couldn't we just leave things as they are—enjoy the fact that we've found each other?' She swallowed. 'I mean—you hardly know me. . .'

'That is something I hope to remedy.' The *Baron* smiled faintly, and lifted her hand to his lips. 'I hope that you will stay here with me, take your place as my daughter, my heiress.'

Rohan moved swiftly, restively, his lean body tense as a coiled spring. There was total silence in the room. Everyone was waiting for her to speak, to smile — to submit.

At last, she said, 'I'll visit you regularly, I promise, whenever I can get away. But I can't stay here. I have a life — a career in England, and I have to get back to it. I think you should stick to your original plan when you dispose of your property.' She looked swiftly and expressionlessly at Antoinette, who glared back at her. 'I came here for some answers. Nothing else.'

Rohan said, 'It's not as simple as that, Sabine.'

She shrugged. 'That's unfortunate. Because I don't want La Tour Monchauzet. There are too many con-notations — too many strings attached to it.' She gave a small, brittle laugh. 'Besides, I don't really see myself as a *vigneronne*.'

'You could learn.' Rohan's voice was harsh suddenly.

She didn't look at him. 'I think I've had enough lessons for a while. I need the life I know, the life that I've made, and that belongs to me.'

There was a tap at the door and Jacques came in. 'The doctor is here for Madame de Rochefort.' His voice and manner was subdued.

'Of course. Ernestine — Antoinette, will you help my wife to her room, if you please?'

The *Baronne* dragged herself to her feet. 'It was for you, Gaston,' she said tonelessly. 'All of it was for you.'

'I understand, *ma chère*. We will talk tomorrow — when you have rested a little.' He sounded kind, but remote.

Don't withdraw from her, Sabine wanted to cry out. She needs you. Don't shut her out and turn to me, as you did with Isabelle. All she said quietly was, 'I think I'll go back to Les Hiboux now.'

'Your place is here,' her father protested.

She forced a smile. 'At the moment, I don't really feel that I have a place anywhere. I need to be alone for a while — to think. I still can't really believe everything that's happened.'

'But you will come back tomorrow.' He was clinging to her hand, and she gently disengaged herself.

'Yes,' she said. She could guarantee that, if nothing else.

She waited until the *Baronne's* sad little procession had left, then started for the door. Behind her, she heard Rohan say something low-voiced and fierce to her father, and then his footsteps following her.

Her throat closed up in misery and panic. As the door of the *salon* shut behind them, she turned on him.

'I thought I said I wanted to be alone.'

'I did not realise,' he said slowly, 'that I was involved in that total exclusion.' He shrugged. 'But it doesn't matter. Tomorrow, life begins again. No more shadows — no more secrets.' He smiled at her, and his hands came down on her shoulders to draw her towards him. 'Tomorrow,' he promised softly, 'I will show you my world — our world that is to be.' His smile widened into a grin. 'Perhaps I can persuade you that the life of a *vigneronne* has much to recommend it after all.'

'No.' She recoiled from the beguiling warmth of his hands, his eyes. How sure he was of himself, she thought bitterly. How sure of her, too. 'It's not going to happen.'

The smile faded, and was replaced by a frown. 'I don't think I understand.'

She squared her shoulders. 'I don't belong here. I'm an intruder—an interloper. I don't want La Tour Monchauzet, or any part of it. Let Antoinette have it, just as everyone always planned.' She paused. 'And you can have Antoinette.'

There was another long silence. He stared at her. 'You don't mean that,' he said slowly, at last.

'Oh, but I do,' she said fiercely. 'My—father doesn't have to acknowledge me. After all, up to a few hours ago, he never knew of my existence.'

'But all that has changed now. . .'

'No.' Sabine shook her head fiercely. 'I—I won't desert him. I've given my word on that. I'll write—and I'll visit him regularly, but I'm going home to England—to stay. To get on with my life. My real life.'

'And what about our life?' he asked harshly. 'Our plans?'

She looked down at the door. 'They—never really existed. I let myself get caught up in a legend—a fairy-tale. Everyone's entitled to one wild escapade—one romantic fling in their life, surely.'

'Is that all it was to you?' His voice was expressionless.

'Yes, of course.' She forced a bright smile. 'Oh, it was wonderful—at the time. You're incredibly attractive, as I'm sure you know. You'll be a—very hard act to follow.'

'Thank you.' His voice was a sliver of ice, a whiplash across her quivering senses.

She swallowed. 'But sooner or later one has to come back down to earth,' she went on. 'Wake up from the dream, and return to reality. Once I've left, everything will settle down again very quickly.' She shrugged. 'After all—life goes on. And I've done enough damage here already.'

'Well, we can agree on something at least,' he said grimly. 'What do you want me to do, Sabine? Go on my knees? Beg you to stay?'

'No.' Panic closed her throat. This was the worst kind of torture, she thought achingly. She was hungry—starving for him. He was standing so close to her that she was aware of the warm scent of his skin. One step, and she could be in his arms, where she craved to be.

But that would be to deny all reason—all common sense. She had allowed herself to be deceived—carried away by his physical allure already. For her own peace of mind—her emotional sanity—she couldn't let it happen again. Because it was her potential inheritance he wanted, not her, and she had to remember that, however much it hurt.

She said huskily, 'Please don't make things more difficult than they already are, Rohan. It was—good while it lasted, but it was all too much, too soon, and now it's over.'

She paused, almost desperately. How gullible she'd

been. How naïve, to think that Rohan could fall in love with her.

'It was just a dream.' Her voice cracked. 'Because things like this just — don't happen. Not to people like me, anyway. . .' Her voice died away into an endless silence.

He did not even move. When eventually he spoke, his voice was flat.

'No,' he said. 'You are right. They — just don't happen.'

He took her hand, raised it briefly and searingly to his lips, then walked away.

CHAPTER TEN

SABINE parked the car outside the château's main entrance, and took a deep breath. This was the moment she'd frankly been dreading.

But I've come this far, she thought. I might as well make it the whole way.

She took a deep breath, then walked reluctantly to the massive door and rang the bell. It was answered promptly by an unsmiling Ernestine. Sabine was surprised to see her. She'd imagined the woman would have wanted to accompany Héloise de Rochefort to the private and expensive clinic in Switzerland where she was having treatment for her nerves.

In the circumstances, I can't expect a warm welcome, Sabine thought wryly, as Ernestine silently accepted her light wrap, then conducted her to the *salon* where Gaston de Rochefort was waiting.

'So you came after all.' He rose from his chair and embraced her warmly. 'I was afraid you wouldn't.'

'I had second thoughts,' she admitted candidly, her answering smile a little pinched. 'But I promised Marie-Christine I'd be here for her wedding. Besides. . .' She hesitated.

'Besides, you promised to lend them your house for their wedding night,' he completed blandly, and laughed at her frank astonishment.

'How did you guess? It's supposed to be a deadly secret.'

'No one will find out from me. I think young couples should enjoy their privacy uninterrupted by cauldrons of soup.' He offered her the chair opposite his own, and looked at her critically. 'You have lost weight.'

'Have I?' she prevaricated. But she knew he was right. It showed in her face, in the starkness of her cheekbones and the deeply shadowed eyes.

'What have you been doing?' He sounded concerned.

'Working,' she said. She'd been glad to find so much work waiting for her when she arrived back in England. It had always proved a solace for past unhappiness, but this time its charm hadn't worked. She'd thrown herself into it with gritted teeth, recklessly taking on more than she could handle. Anything—anything to stop herself thinking.

'And thinking,' she added.

The *Baron's* brows drew together, but he didn't jump to the immediate conclusion she'd feared.

'You must not blame yourself,' he said. 'It was right for the truth to come out. We all treated your mother very badly. It is time amends were made.'

'In spite of the cost?' she asked wryly. She'd been shocked when she'd heard Héloïse was receiving treatment, even though Gaston's letters had been positive and optimistic on the subject.

Her father nodded slowly. 'In spite of that.' He paused, then lifted himself out of his chair again. His doctors were amazed at the speed of his progress, but

he still found some movements awkward on occasion.
'May I offer you an aperitif?'

Sabine requested a *pineau de Charentes*, then sat
back in her own chair, trying to relax, but it was
impossible. Her senses were too finely tuned, listening,
waiting for another footstep, a voice, a breath of male
cologne in the air.

The thought of having to face Rohan again had
nearly kept her in England. Seeing him at the wedding
was something she could bear. There'd be so many
other people around that she'd be cushioned to some
degree from the effect of his presence, she had reasoned. She could hide in a crowd. But an intimate
dinner at the château was another matter altogether —
because this would be the first time she'd as much as
set eyes on him since he'd walked away from her
outside this very room on that awful night.

She'd left for England two days later, having spent
most of the intervening time with Gaston. But Rohan
had not put in so much as a token appearance. It was
almost as if he'd vanished into thin air. Pride and hurt
wouldn't allow her to ask where he was, and Gaston
had volunteered no information, so it had remained a
mystery.

To her shame, she'd postponed her departure to
Bordeaux until the last possible moment, hanging
round Les Hiboux, hoping against hope that he would
come there to find her — to say a formal goodbye at
least, even if she could hope for nothing else, she'd
thought achingly.

Even at the airport itself she'd maintained a fantasy
that he would appear from nowhere, and prevent her,

somehow, from getting on the plane. It was pitiful and degrading, and she knew it, but she couldn't help herself. She wanted — needed him so much, in spite of everything, that it seemed as if her entire heart and soul were crying out to him.

If he'd loved her — if he'd cared for her even marginally, he would have been there, she had told herself, weeping inwardly, as her flight was called. That he could let her go so easily was the final damning proof that his interest in her had been prompted by solely mercenary considerations.

It was the heiress of La Tour Monchauzet that he wanted, she thought desolately. Well, she wished Antoinette joy of him. Perhaps the other girl didn't mind being part of a deal over a vineyard. Maybe having Rohan — being his wife — was enough for her, and she didn't mind occupying some secondary place in his affections.

I'd mind, Sabine acknowledged. I'd want all the love he had to give.

Since her return to England, her existence had been little more than a living nightmare. Rohan filled her mind, sleeping and waking. Her spirit wept for him, while her body ached in deprivation. It was as if she'd been given a glimpse of paradise, and then had it barred to her forever.

She was a fool, and she knew it. Rohan had tried to exploit her cynically for his own gain. But not even the acknowledgement of that could make the pain of losing him go away.

She took the drink Gaston handed her with a brittle

smile, and sipped. He resumed his seat opposite her. 'You are enjoying your life in England?'

'Very much.' She lifted her chin.

'I am glad.' He saw her sceptical look and lifted a hand. 'I mean it. I want you to be happy, even if your happiness is not derived from me, and the heritage I have offered you.'

She stared down at her glass. 'That was never possible — for all kinds of reasons.'

He sighed. 'You are probably right. All my life I have tried to manipulate people — bend them to my will. I have learned at last, and bitterly, that I cannot do this.' He paused. 'But I still wish you had accepted my invitation to stay here for the wedding, instead of at a hotel.'

Sabine swallowed. 'It didn't seem right — in the circumstances.'

'I respect your scruples. And you go back to England — when?'

'Immediately after the wedding, I'm afraid. I can't afford to take any more leave for a while.'

'But later, perhaps, in October at the time of the vintage. You might return then? It is always a time of celebration. We give a big party with food and dancing for the grape-pickers and the workers on the estate. You'd enjoy it.'

Pain lanced through her, and her fingers clenched round her glass. 'I — I can't promise. I — I do have my living to earn.'

She heard the door behind her open, and every muscle tensed.

Gaston said urbanely, 'Ah, Ernestine, have you

come to tell us that our dinner is served?' He used a silver-topped cane to assist him to the dining-room. 'We shall be dining tête-à-tête tonight,' he announced, as Sabine's eyes flickered uncomprehendingly over the two isolated covers laid on the massive dining table. 'Antoinette is staying with friends in Paris at present.'

'And Rohan?' The question was totally involuntary. She could have bitten her tongue out for asking it.

'Rohan?' Gaston repeated blandly. 'Why, Rohan has gone back to the Haut-Médoc. He is at Arrancay with his grandfather.' He waved her courteously to a chair. '*Bon appétit.*'

The bedroom looked beautiful, Sabine thought the following morning, as she stepped back to regard her handiwork.

The bed was crisply made up with the be-frilled white broderie anglaise bed-linen which she'd brought specially from England as her gift to Marie-Christine and Jacques. She'd put bowls of fresh flowers everywhere, so that their cool scent filled the room. Later, she would slip back somehow, and put some champagne on ice on the table beside the bed.

Although the threat of having to meet Rohan had been removed, the wedding was still going to be an ordeal for her, and she'd been sorely tempted to plead sudden illness and stay away from the actual ceremony and celebrations. It wouldn't have been a downright lie either, she thought wretchedly. She was emotionally raw and bleeding after all.

Dinner last night had been torture. Gaston had

chatted lightly on every topic under the sun, except the one that was consuming her. She was almost sure this was quite deliberate. He had volunteered no more details about Rohan's departure, and she couldn't allow herself to ask. Stalemate.

She'd been so sure he would still be at La Tour Monchauzet — had steeled herself to meet him again — which made his absence a total anticlimax. She tried to feel thankful. Seeing Rohan, even fleetingly in a crowd, would simply have caused her more pain, especially at a wedding with all its attendant might-have-beens, she told herself forcefully.

But that was nothing to the agony of never seeing him again, her heart replied despairingly.

As she turned away, she caught a glimpse of herself in the bedroom mirror, and paused to take a longer, critical look. She'd been slender before. Now she was positively skinny, a fact which the dark red silky dress with its cross-over bodice and wrap-around skirt did little to conceal. A sleepless night had added to her pallor and the haunted look in her eyes. She'd hoped the dress could give her some colour. She'd chosen it for that reason — and because it was the colour of wine. The '86 vintage, she thought.

She put the key to Les Hiboux under a stone on the terrace as arranged, and drove to the *mairie*. The farms and houses around La Tour Monchauzet had all festooned their fences, walls and hedges with garlands of paper flowers in pastel colours. The road into town was bright with them.

This, Gaston had told her last night, was a local custom which indicated the popularity of the bride in the community. Marie-Christine must be riding high in local esteem, Sabine thought as she parked her car in the square, and walked up the steps to the *mairie* with the other guests.

Marie-Christine was beautiful in her billowing gown, and both she and Jacques looked almost incandescent with happiness.

Sabine had expected the civil ceremony conducted by the mayor to be a formal, rather bureaucratic business, but it was very much a family affair, celebrated among neighbours who had known the bride and groom since birth.

It was followed by a lunch party at a local restaurant where the tables had been placed outside in the cobbled square. A superb *pâté de foie gras* with truffles was served first, and the main course was *confit de canard* — duck crisp and succulent from having been preserved in its own fat. Then the entire party walked to the parish church for the religious ceremony.

Sabine found Monique at her side. The older woman squeezed her arm. 'It is good to see you again. But what has happened to you?' She tutted. 'You need good food, wine and sunshine to put the roses back into your face. And love, of course,' she added archly. 'We shall celebrate your wedding next, I suppose.'

Sabine forced a smile. 'That's — not very likely.'

'No?' Monique looked genuinely astonished. 'But I do not understand. When Rohan left as he did, we thought — we all assumed that he had gone to prepare your home together at Arrancay.' She stopped, biting her lip. 'Clearly, we were all mistaken. I am desolate.'

She sighed. 'But then, it is never prudent to settle the affairs of others.'

'Now I don't understand,' Sabine said, after a startled silence. 'Are you saying that Rohan has left La Tour Monchauzet for good — gone back to Arrancay — to live?'

'But of course. That was his intention from the first. It is his heritage, after all.'

'But I thought he wanted La Tour Monchauzet.'

Monique shrugged. 'It is a valuable property, and he was needed there while *Monsieur le Baron* was infirm and Jacques was learning to make wine,' she returned. 'But it cannot compare with Arrancay. A truly great vineyard,' she added with a respectful nod.

'Rohan felt for a long time — a tug of loyalty between his grandfather, and the de Rochefort family. They exerted much pressure on him to persuade him to stay. But since this sudden, amazing improvement in the *Baron's* health there was no reason for him to remain.

'Rohan obviously felt he could make plans for his own future, at last. Especially now that his grandfather is no longer as robust as he once was, and needs him at Arrancay.'

She shot Sabine a swift, shrewd look. 'This is a small community, you comprehend. There has been — much talk, naturally about the — changes at the château.'

'Naturally,' Sabine agreed in a hollow tone, her mind whirling.

The church was old, dark and redolent of the incense of centuries. Statues of unknown saints looked gravely down from their alcoves as Jacques and Marie-Christine knelt reverently before the altar.

Sabine tried to concentrate on the intricacies of the unfamiliar service, but all she could think of was Rohan. Rohan at Arrancay. Rohan, contrary to everything she'd been led to believe, turning his back on La Tour Monchauzet.

What could it all mean? she wondered frantically. Her father had spoken sadly about his ultimate failure to manipulate people to his own ends. Was it Rohan he had meant?

I was so ready to think the worst of him, she wailed inwardly. I never gave him a chance to explain—to tell me his side of things. We should have talked together—hammered the whole situation out. Instead, I listened to Madame de Rochefort and Antoinette, of all people. I was jealous and confused, so I let them twist me up—distort everything. What kind of love—what kind of trust was that?

And now he's gone, and I've lost him forever, just as I deserve.

When the ceremony was over, Sabine slipped away from the congratulations and laughter, and the clicking cameras outside the church, and drove back to Les Hiboux.

She needed desperately to be alone for a little while—to think. The house seemed to put comforting arms around her, as she wandered from room to room. But she couldn't bear to go back into the bedroom, with all its bitter-sweet memories, so she left the ice bucket with the champagne in the *salon*.

He seemed to be in every room with her. She heard the murmur of his voice, the whisper of the laughter they'd shared, experienced again the warmth of his arms which had held her with such tenderness and passion.

The urge to get in the car and drive to Arrancay, wherever that was, tempted her almost overwhelmingly, but she suppressed it. She had no reason, after all, to believe Rohan might welcome her reappearance in his life.

She had dismissed him quite brutally, relegating him to the status of a passing fancy, or less. She'd even told him to take La Tour Monchauzet and Antoinette with it, she recalled, wincing.

Rohan was a proud man. How could he forgive or forget such a slight? He'd probably dismissed her altogether by now as fickle, shallow and all too easily swayed by other people. He had his own life — the life he'd offered her. There was no place for her in that life now.

She would sell Les Hiboux, she thought. When the wedding was over, she would talk to Monique, place the transaction in her hands. She didn't need the house, or its memories. When she came to France, in future, she could stay with her father.

Gaston needed her. Their relationship had to be nurtured — the healing process encouraged. Perhaps, in time, his wish to acknowledge her as his child — already an open secret in the locality — could be fulfilled. But not yet. They had a long way to go before that could happen.

The wedding party was in full swing when she arrived back at the château. Music and laughter was spilling from the grand chamber. Exuberant groups of guests were dancing on the terrace in the evening light.

Sabine pinned on a resolute smile and joined them. Gaston was occupying a high-backed chair in the place of honour, and she went to stand beside him, watching Marie-Christine, the skirts of her dress looped over her arm, being whirled round the floor by Jacques.

'Where have you been, little one?' His eyes searched her face. 'I was concerned.'

'I had one or two things to see to,' she returned lightly.

The dancing had stopped momentarily, and a space had been cleared round the happy couple. One of the men was passing round a big china bowl into which money was being thrown, and as Sabine watched Marie-Christine began, with raucous and vociferous encouragement from the men, to lift her skirt demurely and reveal more and more of one shapely leg.

'They are paying to see the bridal garter,' Gaston explained with amusement. 'But watch. . .'

The basin went round again, and this time it was the laughing women guests who were contributing, with squeals of mock protest, urging Marie-Christine to lower her skirt again.

'The prettier the bride, the more money goes into the bowl,' said Gaston. 'The men pay to look. Their wives pay to stop them.'

'I can imagine,' Sabine commented drily.

Everyone was in a circle now, dancing to a rollicking tune played by the small band, and changing partners. One of the younger men charged up to Sabine and pulled her into the circle. She didn't know the steps, but it didn't seem to matter. She found herself dancing with Jacques. Grinning, he swung her round, almost lifting her off her feet.

'*Bonne chance,*' he called out, pushing her, breathless and giddy, towards her next partner.

Gasping, Sabine found herself in other arms, steadied by another body. She opened dazed eyes and looked up into Rohan's face.

Music, voices, laughter faded into some void.

She said his name, and her voice cracked.

The tempo around them had changed to a waltz. His arms held her closely, guiding her to the rhythm of the music. Her throat was dry. She said, 'I didn't think you'd be here.'

'I didn't intend to come. But I owed it to Jacques and Marie-Christine. They're friends of mine.'

She was silent for a moment, then, 'They tell me you're living at Arrancay now,' she ventured.

'Yes.' His tone told her nothing.

Her eyes searched the dark enigma of his face. She said in a low voice, 'I thought you wanted La Tour Monchauzet.'

'I know what you thought.' His voice was savagely derisive. 'But you were wrong.'

She flushed. 'I know that too.'

'*Bravo*. And that, of course, makes everything fine.'

'No,' Sabine said wretchedly. 'I'm not stupid enough to think that. But I want you to know that—I'm sorry.'

He shook his head. 'I was wrong too when I thought you needed my protection. You didn't. You're a real de Rochefort, my beautiful Sabine. You hardly had to learn a thing. Like the rest of the family, you assumed

I was for sale. That my greed for this house — this vineyard was all that mattered to me.'

'You told my father who I was,' she argued defensively. 'Why — if you didn't want him to claim me — to make me his heir?' Her eyes were enormous as she stared up at him.

His arms tightened round her almost painfully. 'I thought he had a right to know, but I didn't want you to be told, not immediately. I said that I was going to take you away to Arrancay with me — and keep you there away from all the bitterness and the lies. I wanted to maintain the fiction that you were Fabien's daughter — until we were married at least, and I felt you were safe enough — secure enough in my love to be able to face the real truth. Gaston agreed, reluctantly. He also had — ground to prepare. Unfortunately Tante Héloise had heard us talking, and decided to intervene. She ruined everything.'

She said in a small voice, 'She told me that you only cared for the vines. That you'd have married Antoinette to possess them. She — wasn't the only one.'

'She was obsessed with Antoinette.' Rohan was dismissive. 'In her mind, she'd twisted her into the daughter she and Gaston never had. And she was determined that I was going to fall in love with the girl. I couldn't convince her that it would never happen, although God knows I tried — with both of them.'

'But you loved the vineyard here — you were so proud of it.'

'I was just a caretaker, until my successor could be trained,' he said more gently. 'I looked after the vines here for Fabien's sake, that's all, because he asked me to. But I never wanted it for myself, in spite of what everyone thought. And in spite of all the inducements I was offered to stay.' His mouth twisted. 'You, of course, were the final one — the one your father thought I would be unable to resist. I'd forgotten his passion for manipulation.'

She stared up at him. 'You'd still have refused?'

'Naturally.' Rohan looked down his nose at her. 'I don't need to marry an heiress, *ma belle*. Like you, I had my own life to return to, and I couldn't wait. My God, I'd even told my grandfather that I was coming home — and bringing my future bride.'

'Why didn't you tell me all this — at the time?'

'I was going to,' he said. 'But before I could say anything I discovered suddenly that I'd meant nothing to you but an unimportant little romantic adventure,' he added bitterly. 'After that no explanations seemed warranted.'

Sabine winced, biting her lip. 'Rohan — I. . .'

'Oh, I knew you'd be deeply disturbed by everything that had happened,' he went on, unheeding of her faltering intervention. 'I expected that. But I thought you'd turn to me for comfort — for reassurance. Once we were at Arrancay together, I thought we'd be able to talk it out — decide what was best for the future. Only you made it clear that we had no future.'

He shook his head again. 'I think that was the worst moment of my life, even worse than realising that poor Héloïse had gone after you — and how near the edge she really was.'

'I was near the edge too,' Sabine said quietly. 'I'd had one ghastly shock after another.' A little sob rose in her throat. 'Oh, I know I should have trusted you — had faith in you — and not listened to other people. But it had all happened so quickly — and I knew so little about you — except that I'd fallen in love with you.'

'I thought that was enough,' he said. 'It was for me. But it was foolish — unreasonable of me to expect. . .' He gave a quick, sharp sigh. 'But why speak of it? It's over now. And I shan't make the same mistake again.'

The last tiny flicker of hope seemed to die inside her, and as it did all the lights in the grand chamber went out. The music faded in discord, and squeals and shouts resounded from all over the room.

'What is it?' Sabine managed to ask past the paralysing constriction in her throat. 'Has — has there been a power failure?'

'A deliberate one,' Rohan returned. 'This is the moment when the bride and groom slip off to their chosen hideaway for a little privacy. Until the *tourain* reaches them, of course.'

'Are they always found?'

'Not always. It takes a long time to visit every house in the neighbourhood — and enjoy some hospitality while one is there.'

The lights came on again, and, laughing and jostling, the guests began to stream towards the door.

'Come on,' someone shouted. 'They'll be at Jacques's brother's farm.'

Sabine found herself travelling in the same direction, Rohan's arm firmly round her shoulders. She tried to hang back. 'No.' But Rohan's arm was like a steel band round her waist, half lifting her from her feet, and carrying her inexorably to the door.

'I don't want to find them,' she protested. 'I want them to have some privacy.'

'Quite right,' Rohan approved. People ran past them, whooping joyously, making for the cars parked outside the main entrance. The night air was filled with the blare of motor horns, as the hunt moved off. 'I think we should have some privacy ourselves.'

He opened the door of his own car, and deposited Sabine in a heap on the passenger-seat. By the time she'd sat up and pushed the dishevelled hair out of her eyes he was behind the wheel, and the car was moving forward.

'What have you been doing with yourself in England?' he shot at her in disapproval, before she could speak. 'Starving for decent food and wine? I can count your bones through your skin.'

'That's none of your business,' she said, off the top of her voice.

'Don't be stupid,' he said reasonably. 'My wife's health and welfare is of major concern to me.'

Her heart began to thump very slowly and painfully. 'I thought you weren't going to make the same mistake again.'

'I'm not,' he said. 'By the time we're married, you will know me as well as you know yourself. There'll be no room for doubts or mistrust ever again.' His smile was crooked. 'Agreed?'

'Yes,' she whispered. She could feel tears of pure joy welling up from the tightness in her chest. 'Rohan—where are we going? Not—not to Les Hiboux, I hope.'

He burst out laughing. 'Is that where the newly-weds

have found sanctuary? Well, no one will look for them there — least of all myself. I wish them a night as perfect as ours, *mon amour*. No, I'm taking you to Arrancay, as I originally planned. Grandfather is still waiting patiently to meet you.'

'But shouldn't we have told someone?' Sabine began to fumble with the seatbelt. 'I have a hotel room reserved. And there's my father. . .'

'Gaston has phoned the hotel,' he said. 'Exactly as he phoned me last night, and told me to come to the wedding.' He paused. 'He was — very persuasive.'

'Oh.' Sabine abandoned the seatbelt, and sat up indignantly. 'I thought he'd stopped manipulating people. What did he say to you?'

'He said that you looked like a little ghost, and tried not to mention my name. He said it was clear to him you were pining away, and that you could only be saved if I took you away and made love to you for the rest of our lives.' He pulled the car into the side of the road, and stopped the engine. 'Perhaps I should start here and now by kissing you.'

Effortlessly, he released the recalcitrant belt and drew her into his arms.

'Oh, yes,' she whispered eagerly, as he bent towards her. 'Oh, Rohan — please — yes. . .'

And, after that, words were no longer necessary for either of them.

PÉRIGORD

The rolling countryside, meandering rivers and unspoilt medieval towns of the Périgord provide a charming atmosphere for modern-day lovers. Its sumptuous food and wine make it the ideal location for intimate candle-lit dinners, while its stunning views are sure to provide you and your partner with a feast for the eyes!

THE ROMANTIC PAST

At the time of the **French Revolution** the old Périgord region was renamed the Dordogne after its 290-mile-long river, and the whole *département* covers an area of 3,500 square miles. The Dordogne is divided into three areas, named by colour: Périgord Blanc, Périgord Noir and Périgord Vert.

The Dordogne area is regarded as the prehistoric centre of Europe. The famous **Lascaux** cave, discovered in 1940, contains some of the most impressive wall paintings in the world, dating back over 20,000 years.

Cyrano de Bergerac, the soldier and poet, whose doomed love for Roxane has been immortalised on stage, and latterly screen, is linked with the Dordogne, and his statue can be seen in the old town of **Bergerac**.

The region is steeped in legend and folklore. For example, as a sign that she intends to be mistress of her home, a bride may still follow the custom of bending the second joint of her finger as the wedding-ring is slipped on to it, thus temporarily halting its progress; at the annual fair held at **La Latière**, unmarried girls drop two pins into the water of the village fountain, looking for them to form a cross as a sign that they will marry within the year; and, owing to November's morbid associations, superstitious couples in the Dordogne avoid marriage during that month!

Banished from the Round Table for love of Guinevere, **Sir Lancelot** divided Périgord among his knights.

THE ROMANTIC PRESENT — pastimes for lovers. . .

The Dordogne is an ideal area for lovers to explore. Since it boasts over a thousand castles, a visit to one of the best known is a must. Why not take a guided tour around the fairy-tale 16th century **Château Monbazillac** before descending to the wine museum in the cellars and indulging in some wine-tasting?

Immerse yourselves in the romantic atmosphere of one of several wonderfully preserved medieval towns in the region. **Monpazier**, **Domme** and **St-Emilion** are well worth visiting; also not to be missed is **Sarlat**, one of the Dordogne's prettiest towns, where you can enjoy the tranquillity of the 17th century public garden and its breathtaking view.

A true city for lovers is **Bergerac**, a charming place where the medieval past blends with a thriving modern town. Take in the sights and sounds of the bustling **markets**, held every Wednesday and Saturday, which sell everything from clothes and jewellery to delicious local produce, and then relax with a walk along the characterful **lanes** of the northern quarter before enjoying a romantic meal in one of Bergerac's many excellent restaurants. The city is surrounded by the famous Monbazillac **vineyards**, producing rich, sweet wines well worth the tasting!

Choosing your meals in this part of France will be an enjoyable dilemma! You can sample local specialities such as the famous **confits** of chicken, duck and goose, preserved in their own fat; also renowned world-wide is the *pâté de foie gras*, traditionally served with Monbazillac wine. Alternatively try freshly caught **salmon**, **trout** or **crayfish**, or deliciously prepared game, complemented by a bottle of one of the Dordogne's well known wines—for example, a Bergerac, Cahors or Pécharment.

DID YOU KNOW THAT . . .?

* the Dordogne is famous for its **truffles**, often still hunted for in the traditional way by trained pigs.

* **walnuts** are one of the region's major exports.

* inhabitants of this part of France are always referred to as Périgordin as opposed to Dordognais.

* the French currency is the **franc**.

* If you want to say 'I love you' in French, say '*Je t'adore*' or '*Je t'aime*'.

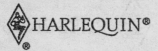 **HARLEQUIN®**

The proprietors of Weddings, Inc. hope you
have enjoyed visiting Eternity, Massachusetts.
And if you missed any of the exciting Weddings,
Inc. titles, here is your opportunity to complete
your·collection:

Harlequin Superromance	#598	*Wedding Invitation* by Marisa Carroll	$3.50 U.S. ☐ $3.99 CAN. ☐
Harlequin Romance	#3319	*Expectations* by Shannon Waverly	$2.99 U.S. ☐ $3.50 CAN. ☐
Harlequin Temptation	#502	*Wedding Song* by Vicki Lewis Thompson	$2.99 U.S. ☐ $3.50 CAN. ☐
Harlequin American Romance	#549	*The Wedding Gamble* by Muriel Jensen	$3.50 U.S. ☐ $3.99 CAN. ☐
Harlequin Presents	#1692	*The Vengeful Groom* by Sara Wood	$2.99 U.S. ☐ $3.50 CAN. ☐
Harlequin Intrigue	#298	*Edge of Eternity* by Jasmine Cresswell	$2.99 U.S. ☐ $3.50 CAN. ☐
Harlequin Historical	#248	*Vows* by Margaret Moore	$3.99 U.S. ☐ $4.50 CAN. ☐

HARLEQUIN BOOKS…
NOT THE SAME OLD STORY

TOTAL AMOUNT	$
POSTAGE & HANDLING ($1.00 for one book, 50¢ for each additional)	$
APPLICABLE TAXES*	$ _____
TOTAL PAYABLE (check or money order—please do not send cash)	$ _____

To order, complete this form and send it, along with a check or money order for the
total above, payable to Harlequin Books, to: **In the U.S.:** 3010 Walden Avenue,
P.O. Box 9047, Buffalo, NY 14269-9047; **In Canada:** P.O. Box 613, Fort Erie, Ontario,
L2A 5X3.

Name: _____

Address: _____ City: _____

State/Prov.: _____ Zip/Postal Code: _____

*New York residents remit applicable sales taxes.
 Canadian residents remit applicable GST and provincial taxes.

WED-F

Travel across Europe in 1994
with Harlequin Presents and...

As you travel across Europe in 1994, visiting your favorite countries with your favorite authors, don't forget to collect four proofs of purchase to redeem for an appealing photo album. This photo album can hold over fifty 4"×6" pictures of your travels and will be a precious keepsake in the years to come!

One proof of purchase can be found in the back pages of each POSTCARDS FROM EUROPE title...one every month until December 1994.

To receive your gift, please fill out the information below and mail four (4) original proof-of-purchase coupons from any Harlequin Presents POSTCARDS FROM EUROPE title plus $3.00 for postage and handling (check or money order—do not send cash), payable to Harlequin Books, to: IN THE U.S.: P.O. Box 9048, Buffalo, NY, 14269-9048; IN CANADA: P.O. Box 623, Fort Erie, Ontario, L2A 5X3.

Requests must be received by January 31, 1995.
Please allow 4–6 weeks after receipt of order for delivery.